✝
R119w

THE WORLD TURNED INSIDE OUT

THE WORLD TURNED INSIDE OUT

GAIL RADLEY

CROWN PUBLISHERS, INC.
New York

Manufactured in the United States of America
Published simultaneously in Canada by General Publishing Company Limited

The text of this book is set in 11 pt. Primer

Library of Congress Cataloging in Publication Data

Radley, Gail.
    The world turned inside out.

    Summary: After his brother has drowned himself and his sister has left
home in anger, fifteen-year-old Jeremy finds himself becoming the last
hope of disappointed parents in a small seaside resort with little to offer
him.
    [1. Family problems—Fiction] I. Title.
PZ7.R1223Wo 1982   [Fic]   82-19796
ISBN 0-517-54616-7

10   9   8   7   6   5   4   3   2   1

For Skip
Thank you, buddy, for your words, your music, which
helped me find my way to this day and this book.

THE WORLD TURNED INSIDE OUT

J eremy! I'm about ready. You dressed?"
"Yes, Mom. Almost."

Jeremy tucked the white shirt into his blue slacks. He ran his fingers through his hair and walked out to the car.

His father, Delbert Chase, was leaning against it, smoking. He glanced wordlessly at Jeremy, knocked the ashes from his cigarette and looked away. Jeremy climbed in the back. The summer heat had settled heavily there and was as smothering as a pillow held over his face. He felt the back of his shirt sticking to the vinyl seat covers.

In a moment his mother, Lydia Chase, emerged from

the house, locking the door behind her. When she settled herself in the front seat, the car sagged slightly toward the curb. His father slid behind the wheel, flicked his cigarette out onto the street and started the engine.

When the first block was behind them, his father began to pick up speed, sending salty ocean breezes back through the open windows. Jeremy looked at his father. The side of his face and neck that Jeremy could see looked tender and raw from his shave that afternoon. There were a couple of red spots where he'd nicked himself. His mother had piled her hair on top of her head, but already little wisps were working loose in the wind and flying around her head like tentacles.

Jeremy leaned against the side of the car and looked out. The streets were getting more and more crowded. Summer vacation had begun a few days ago and people were arriving. The sky was nearly cloudless and, after they found their motels, the vacationers came traipsing down to the beach with their towels, umbrellas, rafts and all the endless paraphernalia they seemed to need.

Listlessly, he thought of Debbie, the girl from Richmond, Virginia, he'd fallen for two years back when he was thirteen. She'd stayed at Baxter Beach for three weeks, and they had been inseparable. He swore that, forever after, he would search for her face among the arriving groups of summer people. But she was unimportant now. That was the thing about Baxter. It was full of changes, comings and goings. Sometimes the important things seemed so temporary.

That hadn't seemed to bother his brother, Tyler. This had been his favorite time of year. He'd liked the girls coming into town. He'd lay back, cool, his face without expression, but his eyes watching, watching. One night Jeremy would see him with one girl; the next night he'd be with someone new. He never seemed to care if they'd go or stay.

In those times Tyler would say Baxter was a stinking little second-rate town. It was true, Jeremy thought. Baxter was sort of a poor man's resort. In his people moods, Tyler often hitched northward to Sand Dune or south to Sunland. They were the real attractions, with their broad beaches of white sand, amusement parks and towering oceanfront motels. The beach was really wasted on the people of Baxter. It was an incidental, a little side source of revenue in a conservative, unambitious town. The beach itself was a narrow strip. The pier looked more rickety each year, and the little food stands and shops along the boardwalk remained in need of paint. Only those who couldn't afford better vacationed at Baxter Beach, North Carolina.

In his hermit mood, Tyler would say Baxter was too crowded. Summer people were everywhere, crawling like flies, ruining the beach, the solitude. Why couldn't his family move to the desert where they could have some peace?

Jeremy had begun to think a lot about peace during the past year. There had been so little of it. But he knew that in looking for peace he wouldn't wander far from the ocean. He'd read about scientists living on the ocean floor for sixty days in something called a habitat. He'd felt a tremor of excitement, thinking of the mysteries they must have unraveled. And there was peace out beyond the breakers. If only it hadn't been tarnished by the memory of Tyler.

At the main intersection, his father turned right—away from the beach. Jeremy thought suddenly how good it would feel to shed his hot, constricting clothes and go leaping into the waves, of how the sun would feel burning down on him, freckling his shoulders. He wanted to shout "Stop! I don't want to go!" But he didn't. He couldn't. Not on this day, especially. The trips on the third Sunday of every month had been as inevitable as the rising of the sun. And this Sunday, the first day of summer, was the anniversary of it all. Even sickness wouldn't excuse him from this. He knew, even if he had been lying in his bed, doubled over in pain, his mother would somehow wheedle him up and out. "If not for your brother, if not for Tyler," she'd say, "for me, because we all have to remember."

Beyond the beach and beyond the strip of rambling old hotels and motels was the town. In silence, they rode through Baxter's other half. It was the half that the summer people seldom saw. There was Flauber's Beach Equipment Supply, puffing dirt clouds from its chimney into the dazzling sky. Everyone just called it the Factory because it was Baxter's only industry. They made beach balls and rafts and other stuff which they sold to stores up and down the coast. A lot of townspeople worked there.

The rest of the town was a collection of low, gray buildings—offices, a few bars and churches. It seemed as if Baxter was trying to carry on as if there wasn't that big, blue ocean just a few blocks off. But it couldn't entirely. The beach tended to spill over into the town. The streets were always a little gritty with sand. Occasionally summer people paraded through the town clad only in swimsuits. They would glance curiously into shop windows at the people in ties or work clothes as if they wondered what they could be doing. Sometimes Jeremy wondered if Mom and Pop didn't resent these people, wishing they had nothing better to do than lounge around the beach getting tan.

At the western edge of the town lay the cemetery. It was a small cemetery. The grass was sparse. The gravestones, except for the newer ones, were wind-worn.

His mother was the first one out of the car. She stared off toward the grave, her shapeless black dress billowing around her plump body like a low tent. Jeremy followed and his father trailed behind them.

She laid the little bouquet of flowers she'd brought on the grave and knelt beside it. Out of the corner of his eye, Jeremy saw her thin lips pressed firmly together. It was odd, he thought. She had never been a churchgoer. But ever since Tyler's death, here she was, every month, as faithful as a deaconess. It was as though Tyler had given her a religion. A religion of mourning. And worry.

Maybe she felt bad because she was always yelling at him. Jeremy remembered one time when Tyler had been sprawled lethargically on the couch and she had yelled, "Tyler, get up off your behind and pick up all that underwear!" Tyler had risen with one withering glance, scooped up all his dirty underwear and stuffed it into the garbage. He had left the house and Mom had to pick all his underwear out of the old coffee grounds and melon rinds. Or maybe she felt bad because she was the one who had called the police on him. They had come for him, and Tyler had ended up in the hospital for months and months.

They all felt lousy about Tyler's death. But couldn't Jeremy mourn in his own way? Could he just remember Tyler in quiet moments and try to understand? No. They all had to follow his mother out here each month. It was like a punishment.

Jeremy stood behind her, staring at the name on the gravestone: TYLER CHASE. The old uneasy, hollow feeling returned to him. Seeing his older brother's name there was almost like seeing his own.

He glanced at his father. His hands were deep in his pockets, his face expressionless. His shirt ruffled out behind him in the wind.

A few yards away there was a canopy over a grave site. Eight or ten old people were gathered around, listening to a minister. They can cope with death better, Jeremy thought. They understand it, expect it. You won't find them dragging themselves here every month to stand over this dry earth and torture themselves with it.

After a time, Delbert Chase touched his wife's shoulder tentatively. "Ready?" he asked.

"No," she whispered. And then more loudly, "NO! It's been a year today, Delbert."

He shrugged helplessly and turned away, picking a path through the gravestones back to the car. He shook another cigarette out of the pack. Jeremy went to stand beside him.

At the grave, he saw his mother dabbing at her eyes

with her handkerchief, and he turned and leaned his head against the car.

The time when grief went ripping through him like a lightning bolt was past. Now there were only the mornings of waking up and seeing the empty bed on the other side of the room, still waiting to be removed. And the nights of sitting out, staring at the stars, with the ocean breeze slapping him in the face. And the insidious messages bleeping through his brain— You were a lousy brother, Jeremy. You never understood. If only you had . . . It went on and on.

In some ways that grief-stricken time had been easier. He had lived in a daze then. There was a wall at which thought stopped. Now that he was fifteen, the wall was crumbling and his mind probed into corners he only half wanted to see.

When at last his mother came, her face was rigid. Her handkerchief was wound tightly around her fingers. She nodded to her husband, and they all got into the car. They rode without speaking for a block and then she broke the silence.

"Tyler was a good boy," she said. "Quiet and mindful. Always seemed to be thinking 'bout things, like a preacher might. I thought he was the smartest of the lot, but it didn't do him no good."

No one replied. They knew about Tyler, what promise he had shown as a child. How proud he had made his parents. And how it all had changed mysteriously during his teens. These things had been said before.

"You're a thinker that way, too, Jeremy," Mom continued. "Never saw two quieter boys. Always thought the girl would be quiet, but she was the one always holler-ing."

Mom shifted in her seat to look back at him with her sharp, dark eyes. "My children let me down. Angela run-ning off to live in some dump. Tyler getting crazy and quitting the way he did. I just pray to God you don't be the same way, Jeremy. What with the way you always took after Tyler."

She turned back and stared straight ahead. She did not expect an answer. She wanted only to leave him with that fearful, infectious thought that maybe brother was like brother, to remind him that he had better straighten up and keep a check on his mind. Jeremy felt the anger flare up inside. So they were alike. She didn't need to keep reminding him. He remembered how everybody had called them Tyler and Tyler Again when they were little. But a little brother was supposed to look up to his big brother and try to be like him, wasn't he? That didn't mean he had to get crazy, too.

He caught the uneasy look Pop gave Mom. But Pop didn't say anything. He never would. He hated to get into any kind of argument, especially with his wife. And maybe he was just a little afraid that Jeremy would get crazy, too. And maybe he figured, like Mom, that if they reminded him and warned him enough, that that would stop him. So whatever his uneasiness was about, Pop let it pass.

Now Tyler and Angela were off the hook. They were written off as the family failures and it was all up to him to make good. Sometimes he felt like Mom and Pop were watching him, waiting to see what he would do. It was hard enough to figure out what to do with yourself without everybody watching. Jeremy closed his eyes until the ride was over.

Once at home, he put on his T-shirt and a pair of cut-offs and headed for the door.

"You hang up your good clothes?" Mom asked.

"Yes, Mom."

"Cleaned up that room?"

"This morning."

"Where you going?"

"The beach."

"It's near dinner."

"I'll grab a hamburger out."

"Always off to the beach. There must be something better—"

"Mom, give me a break. Except for the cemetery, I've been home all day."

She gave him a resigned look, and he slipped out the door.

The summer people were still spread out on their towels, dripping with coconut oil. Little children were darting back and forth, daring the waves. But it was ruined for Jeremy. He couldn't swim now. Instead he walked along the wet sand.

It was like this a year ago, the day Tyler died, Jeremy remembered. Tyler had picked a rotten day to die. You weren't supposed to die when you were only eighteen. And you weren't supposed to die on the first day of summer. If he had to do it, he should have done it on some cold and empty winter day.

Jeremy picked up a thin piece of driftwood and began

to drag it through the sand. The sun hung in the three-quarter point in the sky. People were beginning to stuff everything back into their beach bags and head inland. He imagined them going back to their motel rooms, the women sitting under dryers with their hair wound up in big pink curlers, the men pulling on their flowered shirts. And, in the evening, they'd appear lobster-red in party clothes, to stroll along the boardwalk.

He had to admire Angela in a way. She never took Mom's hassling without dishing some back. Tyler took it, but only for so long. He'd sit still as stone and then, without any warning, he'd do something—like throwing out his underwear—to let you know how he felt. But you had to be giving Tyler a hard time for him to do that. With Angela, you might just breathe at the wrong time and she'd be after you.

Anyway, she finally got what she wanted. For nearly as long as Jeremy could remember, she had been talking about leaving. She'd storm through the house complaining about everything and threatening to leave but never packing. Oddly enough, when Pop went to her quietly and said, "Girl, if you hate us and everything so much, maybe you'd best leave," she just glared at him and retreated to her room.

She finally moved out a week after Tyler died.

That had been a terrible week. Mom took the call from the police. She started screaming and crying on the phone and Pop took it from her. His face gave no sign. He was grim, nodding his head as if the policeman on the other end could see him. They all went down to the police station, Angela and Jeremy still not knowing what for. Mom and Pop came out and told them after they'd seen his body.

Then there was the funeral. It was small. There weren't many friends, and Mom didn't want people to know anyway. She said it was a curse on the family.

After the funeral, Angela was strangely quiet, but her eyes were dark and accusing. Mom cried a lot and yelled about every little thing that went wrong. Pop spent a lot of time at Rosie's Bar. And Jeremy drifted numbly through the days. He wanted to talk about Tyler, but even if he'd known how, there was no one to go to.

Then came the day when Mom went into Angela's room and started yelling. Angela's room was full of plants—on the windowsills, on the dresser and desk and night table—even on the floor.

"I can't hardly see in here for all the plants," said Mom.

"So go somewhere else," snapped Angela. "This is my room. You don't have to see in here."

"Don't sass me," said Mom, the anger rising in her voice. "Long as you're in this house you'll have to keep a room passable. How am I to bring in the clean clothes?"

"Leave 'em outside the door. I like my room the way it is. I wouldn't move a plant."

"I ought to come in here with hedge clippers one day," grumbled Mom.

Angela's voice grew cold. "Don't you dare touch a thing. Didn't you learn anything from Tyler's killing himself? You going to yell at me 'til I do the same thing?"

"Shut up! What are you saying!" screamed Mom. "Tyler's death is not on my head. I only did what a mother has to and no thanks for it. I never heard any sweet words between you and Tyler anyhow!"

When Mom stomped out, slamming the door, it rattled the house. Soon she left for work and, when she returned, Angela was gone—with all her clothing and every last plant. There was only a scrawled note: "I'm going to live in Sunland. Don't bother to come see me. I'd rather be happy. Too bad Tyler wasn't old enough to leave home."

Ahead of him, near the pier, Jeremy saw his favorite spot—an unused lifeguard's chair. He dropped the driftwood and ran to the chair. He climbed the ladder and sat down. The paint on the broad arms flaked away at his touch.

He stared out at the ocean. The waves rose and dashed themselves downward, one after another, like an army of war-torn soldiers flinging themselves upon the beach.

He couldn't help feeling a little betrayed now, when he looked at the ocean and thought of Tyler. The ocean had always been his friend, something constant, with its own words and wisdom. He had always brought his troubles to it and had shed them in it. Now he looked at the ocean and saw Tyler walking into it, his arms outstretched like a young god, summoning the underworld. The ocean had thrown a blanket of water over him and drawn him away into the sleep-filled deep. Then, when the tide retreated, it had spit him back on the shore like a rejected shell.

At first, Jeremy thought it had been all his fault. He and Tyler had been close as kids, but when Tyler reached his teens, he seemed to want things from him that

Jeremy couldn't give—things Jeremy couldn't even understand. There had been a little sense of relief when he heard Angela accuse Mom of driving Tyler to his death. Maybe it wasn't all Jeremy's fault.

But there was nothing to be done anyway. Tyler was gone. Angela was gone. People, events, washed in like the tide and swept away again, leaving him standing alone and empty-handed.

Jeremy leaned back and gazed at the sky. The moon was chasing the sun away. Grayness was veiling the world. He closed his eyes and let the roaring of the ocean fill his ears. The pounding of the waves sounded like the heartbeat of the world. And he felt himself to be a tiny speck, perched on a pile of twigs, clinging to the face of the big, turning world, as helpless as a jellyfish.

2

It was about eleven thirty when his mother found him sprawled out on the front lawn watching the stars. "Jeremy, I want you to get a job," she announced. "Here you are still up and probably slept the day away. It's not healthy. You got some trouble?"

"No, Mom," he said. "I don't have any trouble."

"You put me in mind of Tyler, lying around like there wasn't a thing to be done," she said softly.

Jeremy sat up, suddenly uncomfortable under her gaze. Why did she have to keep comparing him to a dead guy? It was creepy. "It's not that, Mom. It's just nice to lie around thinking and looking at the stars sometimes."

She glanced upward, as if to see if there had been some change in the sky since the last time she noticed it. "The stars'll be there, son, whether you're lying beneath them or working. You work, Jeremy. Best to keep your body busy and your mind from wandering where it oughtn't to be." She paused. "I should've had Tyler working. That's my regret. I set so much on that mind of his I figured to let him have his way and think his thoughts. That's shown a mistake."

Jeremy got up and stuck his hands in his pockets. Seemed like she was wondering whether his mind was slipping away just from his taking a peaceful moment, he thought. You couldn't let Mom catch you just thinking. "I was planning to look for a job, Mom," he said.

"Good. Come on in the house now. I got something to show you."

Reluctantly, Jeremy let the screen door bang shut on the night and stepped inside. He blinked against the brightness of the overhead light and followed his mother to the couch, where she was opening a bag.

"Look," she said, pulling a plastic-wrapped shirt out. "A new good shirt for you. I seen the other's shoulders were 'bout to your neck."

Jeremy pulled it out of the plastic and started taking the pins out. "That's nice, Mom. The other one was getting tight."

She nodded. "Hold it up. There. That looks like it'll fit." She reached into the bag again. "And here—here's a new tie. I was looking in your closet this morning. You've sprouted up so in the last couple of years and all you've got are those little-boy clip-on ties."

"Yeah, I guess you're right," he said, trying to remember when he'd last worn a tie.

"It's a man's tie. You've reached your full height, I think. It'll still look good on you when you're grown."

"It's real nice. Thanks, Mom." He took the shirt and tie and started toward his room. "Think I'll turn in."

"Good idea. But leave that shirt here. I want to iron it for you."

"Aw, Mom, you don't have to. It's late."

"Sure I do. It's full of creases. You couldn't wear it like that."

He smiled and gave her the shirt. She was as anxious as a kid about her presents. Too bad it wasn't a T-shirt or a western shirt—something he could really use. The cemetery—that was about the only time for a plain white one. And with the tie the heat would be unbearable.

"Go on—get your sleep now," Mom was saying.

"Okay. G'night."

When her sharp voice cut into his dreams the next morning, it was something of a shock. He yawned and rubbed his eyes. The clock said 6:10. His mother had been working the evening shift at the hospital, but she must be switching to the morning shift today, otherwise she wouldn't be up so early. Seemed she'd just get settled into one shift and they'd pull her onto another. Seaside was a mental hospital and the aides got stuck with all the dirty work, so people were always quitting and his mother was always having to fill in somewhere.

"Jeremy! Jeremy!" she was calling. "You up?"

"Yup." He pulled himself out of bed and opened his door. His mother was in the kitchen drinking her coffee.

"I was gonna get up," he said. "Just not so early."

"Hmph!" she grunted. "And I'll be off at work, not knowing if you're sleeping or what. Come here and get some breakfast, so I know you're really awake."

"Mom, there's nothing even open this early. I can't get a job until the stores open up."

"Being early makes a good impression. Get yourself a good job, Jeremy. You should be laying money aside for when you're grown. It wouldn't hurt you to pitch in at home, either."

Jeremy went to the cupboard for a bowl and a box of cornflakes.

"You don't know but that you might be starting on a job you'll keep for years," Mom went on. "Work your way up."

No! thought Jeremy instantly. There's not a job in Baxter Beach that I'd stay on at the way Mom and Pop do. Year after year on the same drudge job! There must be other kinds of jobs. Jobs where you got paid to sit and think. Or work in the ocean. Maybe he could be an oceanographer. But no Chase had ever had a job like that. He wondered if he could do it.

"Mom," he said, "most of the places don't open until nine or ten. It doesn't do any good to sit there for two hours."

"If you're needing something to do, you can mow the lawn this morning."

He frowned slightly and sat down at the table. "Where's Pop?"

"He's working split shift today. They had some kinda convention this weekend. He had to go clean up the building before the folks come in to work this morning."

"I can't ever keep track of you guys."

"You'll do fine to keep track of yourself, young man." She swirled the last bit of coffee around in the cup and drained it. She rose, tugging at the skirt of her white uniform. "Don't you forget now, the lawn and the job."

"Okay."

"I've got to run or I'll miss my bus."

"All right."

The door swung shut behind her. Jeremy took his cereal to the living room and listened to the clock ticking on the shelf. On either side of the clock were pictures of the kids. On the left there was Angela's high school graduation picture. Angela was lanky and sharp-boned, like their father, only she did not have his quiet, slow-moving manner. Instead, she had the worrisome energy of their mother. To the right of the clock was a picture of Tyler when he was fifteen—a junior high picture. Unlike Angela's glass-covered, gold-framed picture, it was framed in cardboard. Tyler had missed getting his high school picture taken. He'd gone to twelfth grade for three months. Then he'd gone to Seaside. He'd stayed only a couple of days. The doctors transferred him farther inland to Tennerville Psychiatric Center, so he wouldn't be where his mother worked. He'd come home six months later, just as school was getting ready to close. Two weeks later, he was dead.

Finishing the cornflakes, Jeremy remembered Pop telling Tyler to get a job a few years back, but Mom had said, "No. Let that boy be. He's got his mind on better things than washing dishes and sweeping floors." Pop

(18)

just grumbled, "Sweeping floors has put food in our mouths a good many years," and let it go. Now Mom was singing another tune.

Tyler had wanted a different kind of job, too. For a while, Jeremy remembered, he had wanted to be a doctor. Maybe they had all discouraged him. But he seemed to go at things in such a weird way. Like the time he started collecting frogs. He must have had twenty or thirty of them in a box in their room.

Angela walked in and found him with a frog cut open on his dresser top. He was poking at its heart.

"Tyler! What are you doing?" she screamed.

"Quit breathing over my shoulder. You're getting germs on my patient."

"Stop it, you idiot! At least kill the poor thing first."

"Shut up. You think they kill heart patients before surgery?"

Jeremy heard the argument and followed Angela in. He looked over Tyler's shoulder and saw the frog's legs kicking spasmodically. His stomach churned. "Tyler," he said softly. "That really is gross. You don't have to do that."

"Shut up, both of you! And get out!" He turned his glazed and angry eyes on them and they retreated.

Later, when Tyler slept, Pop had come in and emptied the box of live frogs into the yard. Tyler had been furious when he found out. He caught all the frogs he could, built a fire in the backyard and threw them in.

Jeremy set his empty cereal bowl on the coffee table and got up to look at the pictures. His own junior high school picture had been set next to Tyler's just a month ago. It was eerie how they resembled each other. The same long, thin bodies. The same curly black hair and thin faces. In the picture, Tyler's hair was combed flat against his head, but later he'd let it frizz out so that he'd looked like a mad scientist.

Jeremy's hair was longer now than Tyler's was at his age. But in the two pictures, both of them at fifteen, they might have been twins. There was something different about Tyler, though, Jeremy told himself. He was more excitable, like Angela. More dramatic. Or was that something he, Jeremy, had imagined? Something to explain and put some distance between himself and his dead brother? He shrugged off the thought and went to dress.

The ragged square that was their lawn was easily mowed in a few minutes. Jeremy slipped his harmonica in his back pocket, slung his sandals over his shoulder and headed for the beach.

It was still too early for much activity. There was a small group of surfers in wet suits, paddling their boards out into the water. The tide was still pretty low and they drifted there, some straddling their boards, others flat on their stomachs, waiting for a good wave. They were probably beginners. Soon they'd realize they'd come at the wrong time and give it up.

Along the shoreline, the sandpipers skittered back and forth, searching for breakfast. Jeremy sat down where the sand was dry but the waves could lick at his feet. He pulled his harmonica out and, cupping his hands around it, blew into it. Its lonesome wail seemed to suit the ocean.

After a while, the swimmers began to appear. Radios

clicked on around him. A group of children began building a sand castle. Jeremy looked up toward the boardwalk and saw that it was beginning to come to life. He pocketed his instrument and walked toward the shops.

Sitting on the bench to put on his sandals, he saw Mario rolling out the awning at the pizza stand. He'd started to work for Mario last summer. The cheerful young Italian had been good company for Jeremy. Because Jeremy was so young, he had paid him out of his pocket rather than go through the hassle of applications and working permits. He hadn't even known Jeremy's last name. This year it would be easier since Jeremy had gotten his work permit before school let out.

It would be easier except for one thing. Jeremy had walked off that job. When Tyler died, he'd just stopped coming around for two weeks. When he came back, one of the summer girls had replaced him.

"Eh, I'm sorry, kid," Mario had said. "But you got to be here if you want the job, you know?"

Jeremy had nodded. He had thought of telling Mario what had happened, but the lump that rose in his throat bade him keep silent. It was too late anyway. Mario had his helper.

Now he looked at the pizza stand and hesitated. Mario had probably never figured out what happened to Jeremy last summer. Even though Mom and Pop had tried to keep it quiet, it seemed like a lot of people knew. But Mario wasn't from Baxter Beach. He only came in the summer to run the stand. And though he'd probably heard a kid drowned on the beach, he wouldn't have realized it was Jeremy's brother. Just as well, Jeremy reflected. He wouldn't want Mario feeling sorry for him. Or asking him a lot of questions.

But did he have the nerve to ask for the same job he'd walked off of? "Why not?" he said to himself. Mario was a nice guy. It would feel good to be with him again. Maybe Mario would figure he was just a kid then and give him another chance. He walked over to the stand and waited until Mario saw him.

"Eh, Jeremy, how's it going?"

"Okay."

"So what's new? Whatcha up to?"

"Well, I'm looking for a job, Mario. You need any help this year?"

Mario frowned slightly and looked at Jeremy. "Jeremy, you're a nice kid. But last summer you hurt me, cutting out on me like that. Left me in a bind. I gotta depend on my help, you know?"

"Yeah. That's okay."

Mario swiped at the counter with a rag. "No hard feelings?"

"Nah." Jeremy pushed his hair away from his face. He felt dumb for asking. Of course the guy didn't want to try him again. Why should he? He was lucky Mario wasn't sore at him. "See ya around, Mario."

"Okay. Stop back."

Jeremy stuffed his hands into his pockets and walked for a while. He'd always figured he could hold a job and it bothered him that his first one had ended that way. Telling Mario about Tyler might change things, but how did he know Mario would believe him? He might think it was just an excuse. Anyway, he still didn't like talking about it.

Better to simply try someplace else. He hoped Mario hadn't mentioned him to any of the other shopkeepers. Word would travel fast around the small boardwalk. He stopped in front of Hot Dog Alley. He remembered seeing kids working there last summer.

He knocked on the locked door. A man glanced over and shook his head. "Not open," he called, pointing to the sign stating his hours.

"I'm here about a job," Jeremy shouted.

The man wiped his hands on his apron and unlocked the door.

"You ever work before?"

"No, sir."

"How old are you?"

"Fifteen."

"You're not going to be running off to the beach come noon when the sun gets hot?"

"No, sir. I live here. I see the beach all year round."

The man nodded. He seemed to like that. "All right. I'll try you out. Can you start right now?"

"Yes, sir!"

"Good. Sit down over there. You can fill out an application and then I'll show you around. I'll need to see your work permit, too."

Jeremy filled out the application and handed the papers back to the man. He told Jeremy that he'd get the minimum wage, same as most of the boardwalk jobs. Then he read the application and extended his hand. "Okay, Jeremy, I'm Jim Willis. Come behind the grill and I'll show you what to do. First thing every morning is to stock up for the day. You come in at nine-thirty. We open at ten." He glanced at his watch. "That's about ten minutes. Your main job will be to stay at this counter and keep things stocked. If you get a break, you wipe down the tables."

He showed Jeremy around the place and then opened the doors and rolled up the wooden awning that covered the counter. Jeremy wrapped an apron around himself and went to work.

Business was slow for the first half hour. It was mostly people wanting coffee and doughnuts. Jeremy filled the time wiping everything down and checking the supplies again. He wanted to take care of things before the boss had a chance to remind him. This was one job he wanted to hang on to. Not that it was the greatest job around, but it was something. And maybe Mario would hire him back next summer after seeing he could work someplace steadily.

It would be good going home this afternoon and telling Mom that he got a job on his first day of looking. That was lucky considering the season had already started and there were probably lots of others looking, too. Mom would be real pleased.

The pay wasn't anything special, but he hadn't expected much and he didn't need a lot. He could still lay some aside and chip in at home like Mom suggested.

Then he thought of the diving gear he'd seen in the sports shop downtown. Maybe he could earn enough to get that, too. He hadn't paid much attention to the price when he'd seen it—he only remembered how impossible it had seemed to own it. But maybe not. He could pay someone to take him out on one of the deep-sea fishing cruises. Or maybe he'd get on a real diving expedition.

Suppose he discovered a rock ledge rich in rare minerals? Or an unknown type of fish? He'd get a scholarship. The first Chase to go to college. Jeremy Chase, oceanographer.

The rush began around eleven and things stayed busy until about one-thirty. Between then and his quitting time, three o'clock, he had to clean up and set things up for the evening.

At three Jim Willis said, "You put in a good day, Jeremy. I think you'll work out fine."

"Thanks, Mr. Willis."

"Jim."

"Jim. Well, see you tomorrow."

At the edge of the boardwalk, Jeremy pulled off his sandals and dropped onto the sand. It had been a good day. He enjoyed working behind the counter and taking care of the shop. It felt good to be busy.

He timed his arrival home just after his mother's. Give her a chance to come in, unwind, he reasoned, and then he'd roll in—the working man.

When he walked in, she was sitting in front of the TV with her feet propped up and a glass of ice coffee in her hand. She was still in her uniform.

"Hi, Mom," he said. He walked over and gave her a kiss on the cheek. "Mom, I've got great news. I got a job."

She looked up and smiled. "That's great, Jeremy. That's real fine. What job did you get?"

"I'm the counterman at Hot Dog Alley—on the boardwalk."

The smile faded. "I thought you'd look for work in

town. Is that what you wore?" she asked, eyeing the cut-offs and T-shirt, the sandals slung over his shoulder.

He moved away from her. "Sure, Mom. You don't have to dress up for jobs on the boardwalk. Nobody does."

"What do you think I bought that good shirt and tie for, young man?" she demanded.

Suddenly Jeremy remembered Mom dragging out the ironing board late last night. He remembered the crisp white shirt he had glimpsed but not really thought about, hanging on his closet door. She had meant for him to wear those things to the job! "Mom, I didn't know you—"

"Jeremy, I thought you would look for a good job."

"I'm just starting out. That's about as good as you can do when you're fifteen. What have you got against the boardwalk, anyway?"

She frowned. "The boardwalk's for summer people. It's fly-by-night. There's no future there. You get a job as a bagger at the supermarket and by next year you're cashier. Show them you're a worker and next thing you know they're training you for manager."

Jeremy pushed the hair out of his eyes. "Aw, Mom. I don't want to run a supermarket. I want to do something exciting. Like exploring the ocean, maybe."

"You'd best come to your senses. Who's to pay for that? You'd have to be a rich man."

"Oceanographers get paid for it."

She sipped her ice coffee, thinking that over. It was clearly beyond her realm. And although she'd wanted and expected that sort of ambition from Angela and Tyler, Jeremy knew it bewildered her to have her children moving into areas she couldn't understand.

"There'll be college, then, I'll bet," she said with satisfaction. "You'll need a decent job to afford college."

"Well, I can save with this job. It's a start. Besides, I like the boardwalk. I can see the ocean."

"Huh! Between staring at the ocean and the summer girls, you'll get no work done. Probably be fired in a week." She snapped off the TV and headed for her bedroom. "Going to get out of this uniform," she said.

Jeremy's eyes followed her to her room. For a moment he stared at the door that closed behind her. Suddenly everything had turned from great to lousy. It seemed like nothing he ever did was right to her.

On the second day, he met Gina. The counter of Hot Dog Alley ran right into the counter of the Salt Water Taffy Shoppe. If he leaned his elbows on the counter, he could see the workers next door.

In the afternoon, as he paused in his work to gaze out at the ocean, he heard a girl laugh.

"Never seen so much water, right?"

He turned to the smiling girl behind the adjoining counter. "No—I mean, sure I have."

"How long have you been working there?"

"Just since yesterday."

"Oh, I didn't think I'd seen you." Her straight blond hair fell forward over her eyes and she pushed it back with both hands. "I'm usually off earlier, but I agreed to work late today." She grimaced and mouthed the word *boring* to him, and he laughed.

"I get off at three."

"Me, too," she said, brightening. "You going to the beach after?"

(27)

"Yeah, probably."

"Well, maybe I'll see you then."

"Yeah," said Jeremy. He glanced at his boss. "I better get back to work."

At three he stood out in front of the Taffy Shoppe until the girl appeared.

"Hi, hot dog man," she said cheerily.

He grinned. "Hi. You know, I'm off duty, so you're allowed to call me Jeremy. What shall I call you—Taffy or Ms. Shoppe?"

"How about Gina?"

"That sounds reasonable. Want to walk on the beach?"

"Sure."

As she bent to remove her sandals, Jeremy watched her. He hadn't gotten interested in any girls since Debbie, two summers ago. For a long time he had just missed her so much, nobody else looked good to him. Then all the trouble started with Tyler and then the suicide and he just didn't want to go out. Maybe it's time to shake loose of all that, he thought.

She straightened up and Jeremy shifted his gaze to the ocean. As they started across the sand, Gina dropped a piece of green taffy into his hand. "Compliments of the Taffy Shoppe," she said. "A green bean."

"Pistachio taffy."

"Oh, you've had it. I think it's the weirdest thing—green taffy."

He unwrapped the taffy and popped it into his mouth. "Stop by my shop tomorrow and I'll give you a green hot dog."

She looked at him in amazement. "Really?" Then she laughed. "Oh, you're kidding! You never know what you'll get around here, though."

"Where you from?"

"Maryland."

Oh, great, thought Jeremy. Another summer person. How come girls like Debbie and Gina were never from Baxter? "How long you here for?"

"Uh, I don't know. My parents are—deciding." She smiled. "It's sort of an open-ended vacation. Hey, look! Look out there!"

"Where?"

"See the pier. A little to the left and in, to about the third post."

"Oh. They're dolphins. They're friendly."

"Oh. They're the brainy ones, aren't they? The ones scientists are crazy about?"

"Yeah. Once me and my brother were on a raft way out. About three of them followed us most of the way in."

He fell silent a moment thinking about that day. He had only been seven. Tyler was eleven.

"Tyler, we're getting out too far," he had said.

"Don't worry about it. We can swim."

"Tyler, Tyler, sharks!" he screamed, clutching his brother's arm.

Tyler shook him off and laughed. "Don't be a jerk. Those are just dolphins."

Jeremy withdrew in embarrassment. "I knew," he mumbled. "I was just trying to scare you."

Tyler looked at him with sudden sympathy. "A lot of people mix them up with sharks," he had said. "Lie down and let's paddle back in. Be careful—I don't feel like getting wet again."

"You must come here all the time," Gina was saying.

"Huh? Oh, yeah. I live here."

"You live right here in Baxter Beach? You mean there really are people from here?"

"Somebody's got to take care of things when you all go home," he said.

"Well, hometown boy, you should show me around, you know, since I'm a stranger."

"You want the grand tour of Baxter Beach?"

"Sure. Will it take more than twenty minutes?"

"All right, wise guy. Where's your hotel? I'll take you to our roller coaster tonight."

"Uh, meet me in front of the Taffy Shoppe at seven-thirty," she said.

Baxter's roller coaster was unspectacular. Anyone who'd been to Sand Dune or Sunland would probably not admit that Baxter had an amusement park at all. But neither its shabbiness nor its size seemed to bother Gina. She insisted on riding all the rides twice and they competed at most of the games. Jeremy, bragging that he could fill a room with teddy bears from the softball toss, won only a little rubber turtle.

"Okay, champ," Gina boasted. "Watch this." She hurled one ball after another, knocking over each of the wooden milk bottles, and presented Jeremy with her prize bear.

He laughed and gave her a hug. "You're something, Gina!" he said. "Come on. Let's get out of here and go down to the beach."

"Afraid I'll show you up again, huh?" she said good-naturedly. "Okay, I'll go easy on you."

Stepping onto the beach was stepping into another world. The amusement park was filled with signs, voices and flashing lights calling for their attention. But the sounds of the park were lost in the roar of the ocean. Beyond the strip of sand, the waves came tumbling down to be sucked back into the dark vastness. Sea and sky blended until, looking out at it, Jeremy felt he was floating in a great black globe.

They took off their sandals and walked along the shore. Just ahead, a moonbeam lay like a bridge of light across the water. It seemed to reach out to him. If he could walk across it, he could reach the moon, touch it, unlock its secrets. Had Tyler seen such a moonbeam, and thought to walk it, not meaning to die at all? No, he'd forgotten. Tyler went in early in the morning, when the light was first breaking across the sky and only the birds were witnesses. Then the sun rose, all fire, calling the summer people, and the ocean delivered his lifeless body into their arms.

Jeremy's hand accidentally brushed against Gina's and a little ripple of warmth ran up his arm. He reached out and took her hand, then, feeling her fingers intertwine with his, he sighed and pulled her gently into his arms. For a moment they stood there, just beyond the moonbeam bridge, the ocean breeze washing over them. He had waited so long for this moment of peace and warmth.

Then she pulled away. "It's getting late. I'd better get back."

3

Gina would not let him walk her back to her motel that night. Instead, he walked with her as far as the Taffy Shoppe and said good-night there. After she disappeared from view, he went down to the beach and stretched out on the sand, closing his eyes.

He was especially glad about Gina for one reason. Maybe the ocean would begin to feel like his friend again. It had been part of their coming together. Now maybe he could look at it and think of Gina instead of Tyler all the time. But there was so much of Tyler there. They had fished off the pier together as kids. Tyler had shown him how to dig for clams. He'd been so proud the night they had brought home a feast for the family in their buckets.

Tyler had been a good brother. When Jeremy had been humiliated by a group of bullies, Tyler had twisted their words and thrown them back, until they edged away grumbling. And when Jeremy had gotten himself in trouble at home and was unable to explain himself, Tyler always seemed to understand and come to his defense.

Things had started going bad when Tyler was about fourteen, Jeremy remembered.

"Tyler, I saw a half-sunk boat in the cove," Jeremy had said one day. "Want to go look at it?"

Tyler had just looked at him, laughed and walked away.

In the room they shared, Tyler pushed his bed away from Jeremy's and made a wall of his desk and dresser to separate them. There in his little hideaway, Tyler would sit for long periods with his eyes closed. "Are you awake?" Jeremy asked, looking into Tyler's hideaway. Tyler's eyes slowly opened. He gave Jeremy a silent half smile and shut him out again. Maybe that's just part of getting older, Jeremy thought.

After Tyler had gone to the hospital, Mom had come in and "set the room in order," breaking up Tyler's hide-away to push the bed back across from Jeremy's. After she was finished, she had stood with her hands on her hips to survey the effect. "Now this room looks normal again," she had said. "There was no need for Tyler to hide there like a rabbit in a hole. Do him good to live like other people when he comes home."

One time Jeremy saw Tyler sitting out front, gazing up at the night sky, and went to sit beside him. "I won't talk," Jeremy told himself. "If he wants to talk, let him. I'll just sit here and maybe he won't get sore."

Tyler gave no sign that he noticed Jeremy. But finally, he broke the silence. "Jeremy, you ever wonder who the man in the moon is?"

Jeremy nodded.

"Well, it's me. I mean, I'm one of them. I'm from there." He paused. "You know how the moon pulls the tides?"

"Yeah."

"Well, it pulls me, too. When the tide is out, I'm down. When it's in, I'm happy. I always figured I was different. Now I know I'm just here to study you guys."

Jeremy laughed, pleased Tyler would joke with him. "That's funny, Tyler."

"Funny! Funny will be when I take you back there with me. Or maybe cut your throat and just take your soul back!"

Jeremy clapped his brother on the back. "You're crazy, Tyler. Really crazy."

Suddenly Tyler whirled around. "Shut up!" he yelled, storming off. "Just you shut up!"

"Tyler, I didn't mean it that way!" Jeremy protested. "I was just kidding."

There was no reply.

When Tyler was seventeen he asked Jeremy to go to the beach with him one night. Jeremy was thirteen then. Jeremy had all but given up on ever being close with Tyler again. He hoped, at last, he would be allowed back into his brother's world. It was nearly midnight when they crept out of the bedroom window.

"Is this where you go when you go out at night?" Jeremy asked, once they'd gotten beyond sight of the house.

Tyler gave him a sharp glance.

"I hear you leaving through the window a lot," Jeremy explained. "It's okay. I wouldn't say anything to Mom or Pop. I just always wondered where you went."

"Be quiet," said Tyler gruffly. "You talk too much."

They walked about a mile down the beach to the narrow, secluded cove. The little beach was rocky and the water shallow and murky with seaweed. Tyler insisted they collect wood for a bonfire. And when it was hissing and crackling, spitting out sparks into the night, Tyler sat cross-legged in front of him.

"Because you are my brother and the closest one to me," he said quietly, "I want to confide in you. Jeremy, I have received a power. I didn't ask for it, I didn't want it, but it came to me."

"What sort of power?"

"Jeremy, I can see into the hearts of people. I can feel them needing me and my power. I can change the course of events, but I need the people's will."

Jeremy floundered for words. Was Tyler joking, trying to make a fool of him? He would get Jeremy believing and then start laughing, "Ha, ha, jerk, you'd believe anything." Jeremy felt the muscles in his back tightening. They were going to be buddies tonight. A couple of guys sneaking out, and now this. But if he laughed, Tyler might get mad. Everything would be ruined again.

"What are you talking about, Tyler?"

The shadows were moving across Tyler's face as the fire danced. His whole being was filled with intensity. "Jeremy, give me your will and I'll show you. Surrender to me. I need you to live and you me. I need the people to live and they need me. You see, everyone's fate is intertwined with my own, but they do not know it yet. Your fate, especially, is bound to mine, now that I have given you knowledge.''

A chill swept through Jeremy. This was no joke. Tyler believed this stuff. He actually believed it. His brother was crazy, really nuts. Jeremy rose. "Let's go home," he said uneasily. "Tyler, come on. I don't like it here.''

Tyler grinned up at him. "You're scared, aren't you?''

"No. It's late. I just want to think about everything," he stammered. "I'm going home.''

"You are scared. Wait. I'll walk with you. But, Jeremy, remember this, you're my brother. You're the same as me. Don't fight it. Just follow me. You can't help it anyway.''

After that, the distance remained between them. But Tyler's eyes had seemed to follow him everywhere. He had looked at Jeremy almost with pity and there were times that Jeremy, under his brother's scrutiny, had wondered if his will wasn't being slowly taken away.

And now, lying there on the beach, Jeremy felt a haunting remorse. Suppose Tyler really did have a power. Maybe not exactly as he described it, but something he didn't quite understand himself. The world was filled with strange things—psychic phenomena, suggestions of predestiny. Wasn't it possible that Tyler had discovered within himself some prophetic vision and become so overwhelmed with it that he lost his balance? Everyone doubted and denied him, even his own brother. Maybe all he had needed was someone to listen and help him sort out the strange, wonderful things he was discovering about himself. Wasn't that enough to drive a person into the sea?

Jeremy awoke the next morning with the thought that Tyler had been right in at least one respect. His destiny was bound up with Tyler's. Even his mother saw that and thought he would follow in Tyler's footsteps.

But it wasn't quite that way, Jeremy thought. Power or no, something had gone terribly awry in Tyler's life. And who would bear the guilt of that? Jeremy would, because Tyler had come to him, confided his secret thoughts and Jeremy, out of fear, had turned away. Why hadn't he known what to do? Now his own life would bend under the burden of guilt. And for how long?

He sat on the edge of his bed, thinking. On the dresser opposite him sat a carving of a ghostly creature rising out of a piece of driftwood. Tyler had bought it on the boardwalk just before he had gone to the hospital. Most of Tyler's personal things had been packed up or given away. But this piece seemed to have had some special meaning for Tyler, and so Jeremy kept it as a reminder.

But I didn't send him to the hospital, Jeremy remembered suddenly. Mom did that.

Jeremy remembered the day. Tyler had been sent to the hospital while Jeremy was at school. He was told just after he got home. And he accepted it. It seemed to make sense at the time. Why? How come he didn't yell and scream at them for it? His own brother, sent to the loony bin, and he hardly says more than Oh.

Mom made the call, but Pop went along with it, too. What was wrong with this family?

Jeremy set his chin for the argument he felt boiling within him and strode into the living room.

His mother, who would fill in on the evening shift that day, was washing the windows in the kitchen. His father had his head under the sink and was tinkering with the pipes. Jeremy leaned against the living room door frame, looking into the kitchen at his parents' backs. "So what was supposed to be wrong with Tyler, anyway?" he asked abruptly.

His mother stopped wiping the window and turned slightly toward him. From under the sink, the clink of his father's wrench stopped. "You don't say 'good morning' anymore, Jeremy?" she retorted.

"Good morning. What was wrong with him?"

His father began tightening the pipe again, slowly, as quietly as he could.

"You know full well he lost his mind," said Mom.

"What does that mean? Where do you lose a mind? Did everybody go look for it?"

"Don't you be smart, boy. Schizophrenic. That's what they called Tyler, if you have to put a word to him," she continued.

"They called him that," said Jeremy with heavy emphasis, "because *they* wanted to get the money you paid to keep him there."

His father pulled his head out. "Your brother was a very sick boy. Didn't take money to see that."

"And I say we let him down because nobody cared enough to listen and help him!"

"Look, mister," Mom said evenly, "don't tell me about who cared. Caring was sending him to the hospital. You don't think it cost to keep him there?"

Jeremy's heart was pounding now; he felt like he wanted to scream. "You call *that* caring? Tyler was worse when he got out of the hospital. He never tried to kill himself before. Why did you lock him up in that crazy place?"

"Because he belonged there!" she said fiercely. "Tyler couldn't be kept at home any longer!"

Jeremy wheeled and circled around the living room. Then he came back to the kitchen door. "How can you still work in that hellhole after what they did to my brother?" he yelled.

"Watch yourself, boy," said Pop.

There was an electric silence as Jeremy and his mother glared at each other.

"Seaside is a lot of things," she said, "but it is no hellhole. And Tennerville is one of the best hospitals around."

Jeremy forced himself to be calm. "I don't believe it. My brother is dead. I think you say that because you have to."

"Don't believe me, then. Think what you want. I can't make you see it."

"Yeah," said Jeremy, sucking in his breath. "I'm going to work."

When he returned that afternoon, he was glad to find the house empty. He still felt angry, thinking about the argument. He made himself two peanut butter sandwiches and took them out to the front step. The warm salt breeze blew up from the ocean and seemed to clear his head.

Pop pulled up out front and started up the walk.

"Hi, Pop."

"Son." He put his foot up on the step by Jeremy and looked down at him, shading his eyes with a long, thin hand. "That was a pretty tough scene you had with your mother this morning."

"Yeah."

"She felt pretty bad after you left. Then I had to leave for work and I s'pose that didn't help none."

Jeremy didn't answer.

Pop lit a cigarette and sat down beside him. His face gave no indication of his feelings, but his gray eyes were troubled. "It ain't an easy decision to come to—sending your son to one of them places. It kinda tears at something inside you."

"Even worse to be there," said Jeremy.

"I know this thing ain't resting easy with you, either, Jeremy." He hesitated, tugging at the knee of his green custodian's pants, and crushed his cigarette carefully with his heel. "Look, why don't me and you go out tonight? I'll take you by Rosie's. We can get a couple of beers."

Jeremy glanced at his father. The invitation surprised him. They had never gone out, just like a couple of guys together. They seldom even talked about anything important. Suddenly his father seemed concerned. "Okay," he said.

Since the bar was just a few blocks away from the house, they walked. His father walked slowly, as might a man who had never known what it was to hurry. And Jeremy, by his side, was suddenly haunted by a vague feeling that this scene had happened before. Years ago. Only he was behind a screen door, his nose pressed against it. The shifting images fell into place like colored chips in a kaleidoscope. It was Tyler walking, strutting beside Pop, taking two quick steps to one of Pop's. They were going downtown together and he, Jeremy, was being left behind. He was only about five then, too young to be included. Jeremy remembered how the tears burned at his eyes and how he held them back. Tyler would have called him crybaby. He would show them he was big enough to go. But there was no one to see his bravery—only a quick, triumphant, backward glance from Tyler. Pop's hand, reaching out to tousle Tyler's hair, was framed by the wooden door; the image hung in Jeremy's mind.

There was no flashy sign out front of Rosie's Bar, nor was it on a main street. Its loyal patrons were residents of Baxter, not the beach crowd. Originally, the building had been a small frame cottage. But its owner, Cap Rosenburg, converted the downstairs to a bar and lived alone in the rooms above.

The room was dimly lit by a few shaded lamps on the walls and some flickering neon beer signs. From a shelf high above came the gray glow of a TV set. The place was not crowded. There were a couple of men his father's age at the bar, watching the ball game. In the adjoining room, two younger guys were playing pool. The bartender, a tall, round man, was leaning on the counter watching the game with his customers.

His father strode in, greeting the men at the bar. He swung his long legs over a stool, and Jeremy sat down beside him. The bartender spotted them right away and came over. He jerked his thumb toward Jeremy. "Del, is this big kid yours?"

His father grinned. "Yeah. My youngest kid, Jeremy."

(41)

He nodded toward the bartender. "This is Rosie. Rosie, set us up, will ya?"

Rosie leaned on the bar and smiled at his father. "Del, this is a big kid, but he ain't of age."

"All right, all right. Whatya want, Jeremy, a cola or something?"

"Sure."

"Bring us a cola and a brew, then."

Rosie left to get the drinks. His father looked at him with embarrassment. "I'm sorry, kid, I just thought, Rosie being a buddy and all . . ."

"It's okay, Pop. Really." Jeremy would have had the beer. He got the feeling his father really wanted him to. Some sort of man-to-man ritual, he guessed. But he didn't mind being turned down. When he was little he had had beer from his father's forgotten can. The warm stuff had fallen like liquid fire into his stomach. Much later, he had seen drunken guys stirring up trouble on the boardwalk and Tyler reeling into the bathroom one night to hang his head over the toilet. He'd decided then he'd just as soon do without.

Rosie set the drinks on the bar. "You about done with school?"

"No, I'm just starting high school."

"He looks old from thinking so much," said his father with a grin.

Jeremy forced his mouth into a good-natured smile. It was a joke—or supposed to be. But he felt a flicker of resentment. Before they'd come Pop had seemed interested and concerned about his thoughts. Now he was making fun of them. It was because of Rosie, he told himself. Pop didn't like to let people know things weighed on him. Do what you have to and don't complain—that was Pop's philosophy.

Rosie was grinning back. "A thinker, huh? Well, that's good. Make your plans early. That's the way to get ahead. You gonna work with your old man when you get out?"

"No." He had answered too quickly. Out of the corner of his eye he saw Pop shift on the stool and take a drink from his mug. Pop was not as ambitious for his kids as Mom was. It was enough for him that they finish high school and get a steady job. A son who chose to follow in his steps—no matter how humble—would be the ultimate testimony to his success. "I'm not sure what I'll do yet," Jeremy said quietly. "Maybe—maybe study some more."

Rosie slapped the counter edge with his fingertips. "Study and more study. These kids today study on how to keep from working!"

Pop shrugged. "Maybe he won't end up a working stiff like us, Rosie."

"Your old man's right," Rosie agreed. "You go ahead and study all you can. Make a good place for yourself. Just remember your old man's sweat gave you your start." He walked off to wait on some other customers.

Jeremy wrapped his fingers around his mug of cola and looked away from the bar. The air was stagnant and smoke-filled. It made his eyes smart. He wished Pop had invited him for a walk on the beach instead.

One of the pool players came up to the counter and ordered two hamburgers. Rosie put two cellophane-wrapped buns in the small microwave oven while the young man leaned on the counter, waiting.

Jeremy noticed his father looking at the pool player, who hunched his shoulders and turned away. Jeremy was struck suddenly with the thought that Tyler would have been about the age of the pool player. He wondered if Pop was thinking of Tyler, wishing he was out for a beer with Tyler. Tyler had been a drinker and old enough not to get the embarrassing turndown from Rosie. And here he sat with a cola, wishing he was on the beach. It seemed that Tyler had always taken Pop's attention away from him. When they were kids, Pop turned first to Tyler. Older kids were easier for Pop to deal with. And Tyler was an eager student. Always first to hold Pop's flashlight, first to hand him his tools. It must have made Pop feel pretty special. Then, when Tyler became a teenager and rejected Pop, Pop crawled off like a wounded animal, tucking his feelings inside so that Jeremy still couldn't reach him.

Pop took another drink from his mug and tapped his cigarette pack on the bar. He pulled one out, lit up and faced Jeremy.

"This thing about Tyler still got you upset, don't it?"

"Yeah. It bothers you, too, doesn't it?"

"Sure it does. Sure. But what can I do? Tyler's gone. I just got to get up and keep going. Hope for the best."

"Seems to me like we ought to find some answers to it."

"And you think your mother's the answer. That it was her fault."

Jeremy glanced at Pop. And yours, he thought. You

could have stopped her from making the call. "I'm just looking at the results, Pop. What can I think?" he said aloud.

Pop sighed. "Well, it's a woman's place to deal with the kids' problems mostly. Comes naturally, usually. And Lydia, oh, well, I suppose she tried, and I guess she kept thinking that Tyler was smart enough to see his own way clear in things." Pop finished off his beer and motioned for Rosie to bring him another. "But I guess you can't fault somebody for what they don't have."

Jeremy looked at the people talking on the television screen without comprehension. "Pop," he said suddenly. "Do you think Tyler was schizophrenic, like Mom said?"

Rosie set down the beer. Smiling, he started to say something, then caught the look on Del Chase's face and backed away. From the pool table behind them, there was the hollow cracking sound of wooden balls hitting each other. His father stared into the golden liquid. "A man doesn't like to think his son is crazy," he said.

"Mom thinks he was," Jeremy said bitterly.

"Your mother knows more about it than we do, working at the hospital."

"She never studied psychology."

A customer who was seated nearby looked over at them and Pop lowered his voice. "The doctors said so. They studied." He took another long draft of his beer.

"Maybe the hospital wasn't the right thing anyway. Maybe we should've helped him—tried harder to understand him, talked to him."

"You couldn't understand Tyler toward the end, Jeremy."

"Maybe he just needed to hang around home—you know, relax, get himself together."

"We couldn't keep him home. He got too wild." Pop paused. "Listen, son," he said slowly. "It about broke your mother's heart to send Tyler away and it was hell on me. But Tyler was not a regular guy. You don't know everything about Tyler."

Jeremy's eyes met Pop's, and there was a brief jolt of recognition. It was as if he'd never really seen his father before and then, there he was, bared to the soul. It was hard to picture Pop doing anything but silently plodding along—much less going through hell. Had he cried? Beaten the wall? Cursed his luck? Jeremy had always pictured the event as a cold-blooded one—Mom screaming, "I'm calling the police to take this lousy kid to the nuthouse" and Pop, nodding, "Guess you're right, Lydia." Now it was shifting. Mom, her heart breaking. Pop grieving, suffering. He wondered. . . .

But then the veil dropped between them as quickly as it had lifted. Pop sighed deeply and shook out another cigarette. "Jeremy, Tyler stopped going to classes at school. Instead, he'd go to the office and stand at the principal's door. He wouldn't say anything, just stared at him. When they asked him what he wanted, he wouldn't talk. We took him out of school for a while to straighten him out."

"You told me he had mononucleosis," Jeremy broke in. He struggled for the details at that time. Tyler scarcely talked to him then anyway. And Mom and Pop had told him to stay away from Tyler because mononucleosis was contagious.

(46)

"We said that, but it wasn't true. We didn't think you should know about it. Maybe that was wrong. You didn't know, either, how I had to bring Tyler in to bed or he'd stand in the yard all night."

Pop rubbed the creases in his forehead and frowned. "The day we sent him to the hospital, you weren't home. You know what happened that day? He swung at his mother. Why? Because she wouldn't go to the store for him. She goes out to work five nights a week and he can't walk down the street for a lousy jar of coffee."

Jeremy felt like he'd been punched in the stomach. This didn't sound like his brother. Sure he'd gotten intense and distant as a teenager and there was the time with the frogs, but Jeremy hadn't known him to be violent with people. And his father was not through.

"Jeremy, you know what I had to do?" Pop closed his eyes as against some terrible vision. His right hand was clenched in a fist and he wrapped his left hand around it. "I knocked him out. I hit my own son in the face like he was some jerk in a bar. It was the only thing."

Once more the reel turned in his mind. Mom, Pop and Tyler, like actors playing the same scene as written by yet another author. This time Tyler's big, knuckled fist swung out. Mom jumped back, her mouth forming a silent O of surprise. Then another fist—Pop's—connected with Tyler's jawbone, and he dropped like Daniel Boone's bear. Mom on the phone now, hysterically talking to the police. Pop, like a statue, staring at the crumpled body of his firstborn son.

Was Tyler taken to the hospital unconscious, then? Did he wake up in the police car, his jaw swollen and aching and no one to tell him why? Or did he open his eyes at home, reaching out for forgiveness, only to have the handcuffs snapped around his wrists?

His father opened his eyes and gazed at Jeremy. "You know what he brought home from Tennerville? A suitcase full of keys. I don't know where he got them. God only knows what he did with all the clothes his mother bought for him to take."

"I knew Tyler was going through some bad things," Jeremy said softly, "but nobody ever told me any of this."

His father seemed not to hear him. "I did what I could for Tyler. He was my son. When he was young he respected me. Then something happened. Got too full of himself, I guess. I dunno. Your mother, I think she made too much of his brains. A little work might have helped him. Maybe I should have been tougher."

Hot Dog Alley, thought Jeremy, is more than a job. Work is a wonder drug to them. Mom said it, and now Pop. Brains are nice, but you have to sweat to show you're okay. Hot Dog Alley is a symbol of my sanity.

The smoke in the darkened room was suffocating. The talk and laughter seemed to be growing louder. He touched his father on the shoulder. "Pop, I've got to get out of here."

His father peered at him as if from another realm. "You okay?"

"Yeah."

Rosie was sauntering over, grinning.

"Hey, Chase," called a man at the other end of the bar. "I'm taking bets on tomorrow's game—you in?"

Rosie swaying slightly before them, held out his thick,

hairy arms. "Ralph, don't interrupt! Don't you know a father-son talk when you see it? This is a family bar."

The amused glances of the other customers turned toward them. Rosie, sensing his audience, spoke louder. "Jeremy, you want a hot dog to go with your cola? Some potato chips?"

"No, I'm just leaving," Jeremy mumbled. He turned and headed for the door.

Behind him he heard Ralph calling out, "Del, why didn't you bring the little woman, too?" A wave of laughter rose above the chatter.

Jeremy stepped out into the cool evening air and breathed deeply.

4

Maybe Mom and Pop were right. Work attached you to the normal world like a claw. If your grip loosened, you were swept out into the sea of insanity. Wipe a counter. Pour ketchup from the big glass bottle into the red plastic squeezer. Chop onions, blinking away the tears. Onion tears were okay. Work, and think only of work. How many doughnuts could you stack before they began to teeter?

Last night, he had fled the bar to wander the beach. Down to the cove where he and Tyler once sat. It was approaching midnight. He built a fire and sat cross-legged before it, willing himself into the mind of his brother. "I have received a power. I didn't ask for it . . . the people need me, I need them. . . ." And again, with the *feeling* of power. Desperate, yet commanding. But no one is listening. No one cares. They laugh or recoil in fear. My God! Why don't they help me? I'm lost—tossed about in the sea and there's nothing solid to grab on to.

Jeremy rose and knocked apart the fire with a branch. Burning logs hit the water, sizzling and smoking. Then there was nothing but the charred remains and he left.

But today the world was friendly. The ocean was deep blue. The foam that capped the waves reminded him of frothy egg whites. Shiny plastic beach balls were sailing through the air. What could be wrong in a world with red, yellow and blue beach balls?

In Hot Dog Alley the big propeller fans buzzed above him. Behind him there was the comforting smell of grease on the grill.

Jim came out of the back room and began taking raw hamburger patties out of a box. "Jeremy, the hot dog supplier's here. Stack the dogs in the back of the cooler and pull the old boxes forward. I'll keep an eye on the counter."

In the cooler, he hoisted the boxes of hot dogs from the far corner to a new spot by the door. The supplier had left ten new boxes smack in the middle of the cooler. Jeremy reached for the top box and heaved it over to the corner. Reach and heave. Reach and heave. His body swung back and forth like a machine. The coldness of the bleak little room was nice. It drew him into himself. He was numb but functional. He could touch but not feel. A perfect replica of a living being. The humming of the cooler could have been the humming of his own motor.

When he came out of the cooler, his arms still goose-bumped from the chill, the lunch rush had begun. Jim was working like an octopus at the grill. Since he'd had to work the counter, too, he didn't have as many burgers and dogs ready as usual. Customers were waiting in line and looking a little edgy. The sight jolted Jeremy out of his trance and into action. He rushed to the counter and Jim flashed him a grin that said Not a minute too soon!

A barrel-shaped man in a terry-cloth beach jacket ordered ten hot dogs. "One with relish, three with mustard, five with ketchup and one with onions and mustard."

"The fixings are all on the counter for you, sir," said Jeremy. He dropped ten hot dogs in buns, lined them up in a carry-out box and set them on the counter. "Five dollars, sir."

The man paid him and started fixing the hot dogs.

"Now who's next?" asked Jeremy, looking at two boys who were peering over the counter.

"I was!" they chorused, and promptly glared at each other.

"Come on, guys. Help me out. One of you must have been first."

"You came second," said the redhead. "Give me a hamburger with everything."

"But you left to throw something in the trash," objected the blond.

"So what? You want me to litter?"

"Okay," Jeremy cut in. "It's not worth a war. What do you both want?"

"Hamburger with everything and a cola."

"Hot dog and a root beer."

Jeremy fixed the food and handed each boy his at the

same time. As he turned to get their drinks, the barrel-shaped man called to him. "Hey, son, I forgot to order the drinks."

"Be with you in a minute, sir."

"But my hot dogs are getting cold."

"Sorry, sir." Out of the corner of his eye, he saw the man drumming his fingers on the counter and frowning. He delivered the drinks to the boys, took their money and then turned back to the man.

A moment later the man scuffed off with a box of hot dogs under one arm and a box of drinks under the other. Finally, all the customers had been served. Jim, standing by the hot grill, wiped his brow and grinned at Jeremy. "You're pretty good under fire."

"Thanks." Jeremy put his back to the counter. Somewhere in the flurry, he had lost his distance. He had come up like a diver from the deep, broken through the final foot of water and suddenly things were clear and sharp again: the hand-painted navy-blue letters on the menu board, the fly that homed in on a mustard spill by his elbow and the tiny black whiskers that stood out on Jim's face. He hadn't bothered to shave that morning.

"Customer'll test you sometimes," said Jim. "Takes a lot of patience not to bark back at 'em."

"Well, they'll have to try harder than that if they want to get me mad." He wiped up the mustard spill and rinsed out the rag in soapy water. He didn't mind that he'd broken through. It felt good. It wasn't a big job, but it was one that he could do. And he was appreciated. Not like at home.

"Once a guy dropped all five of his hot dogs not a foot

away from the counter," said Jim, "and he thought I should replace them—free!" He scratched the stubble of beard and looked out at the boardwalk. "Get ready. Here come more."

A family with three little kids was approaching the counter. Jeremy turned to wait on them.

When the rush was over, he restocked the condiments, wiped down the counter and refilled the soda dispenser.

"Kid, you got a great future in hot dogs," said Jim.

Jeremy made a face. "Terrific."

"Aiming higher, huh? But where else can you stare at the pretty girls when it slacks off?"

"You got a point there," said Jeremy. "What do you do off-season, Jim?"

"Work at a ski resort in the north. I get the best of both worlds. Keep an eye on things a minute, will you, Jeremy? I'm going to go make out the order for the doughnut man."

Jeremy leaned on the counter and looked out at the beach. A couple of guys were throwing a Frisbee, making it skim along the surf and curve up. The lifeguard stood up in his chair, blew his whistle and waved some swimmers in. At the foot of his chair a group of teenage girls clustered, waiting for him to talk to them again. That was the job to have!

Then he heard Gina talking to a customer next door. "Psst! Got any green beans for sale?" he asked when she was alone.

She leaned across the counter, her long hair shining like golden silk. "Jeremy! It's been so busy, I didn't see you all morning."

"I think there's another convention in town."

"A convention! Here?"

"Even Baxter gets conventions *sometimes,* Gina," he said. "Probably United Nail Clippers' salesmen, or something like that! Want to do something after work?"

She scowled. "I can't. My folks want me to go see some historical spots with them. Isn't that the dumbest thing you ever heard of?"

"The historical spots around here aren't very exciting, unless you really like reading plaques."

"How about breakfast tomorrow? Is anything open early?"

"Yeah. The restaurant on the pier is open at dawn on account of the fishermen. It's not bad."

"Dawn," she said thoughtfully. "You know, I've never seen the ocean at dawn."

"Well, if you can struggle out of bed that early, I can."

A woman called from within the Taffy Shoppe. "This bin of banana taffy is about empty, Gina."

"I'll get it." Then she whispered, "I'll meet you on the beach at dawn."

He was sorry Gina could not provide him with a good reason to stay away from home that afternoon. He'd managed to avoid seeing Mom since the argument and he wasn't sure how to begin again with her.

After his talk with Pop last night, it was hard to see her as a complete ogre. She had suffered, Pop made that clear. And, like Pop said, she just wasn't equipped for Tyler. If only the hospital . . .

"Hello, Jeremy. Glad to see you're still living here," Mom said, wincing at her own attempted humor. "How was work?"

"Fine. How 'bout yours?"

"Oh, good. Hot dogs—don't seem like the place for you, Jeremy. Bright as you are . . ."

"I like it okay, Mom." He poured himself a glass of cola from the quart bottle in the refrigerator.

"Jeremy, I been doing some thinking about a job with more future for you." She adjusted one of the bobby pins in her hair, catching up some of the loose strands. "I talked with Mr. Fielding over to the hospital cafeteria. He said he could use some help."

"Seaside?"

"Yes." She hurried on. "Lottie Jones's boy, Randolph—he got a job in the hospital cafeteria with his mother. After a while he got to be what they call work counselor over some of the patients. Then the state helped put him through school—through college."

"Mom, I *have* a job. I *like* Hot Dog Alley."

"Oh, well, it's a start, I guess, like you said. But you wouldn't be so foolish—you wouldn't pass up a chance—"

Jeremy sighed. It wasn't enough that he'd gotten a job, as she asked. It had to be the job *she* wanted. Why was she always pushing?

"Jeremy, it's seven to three, no weekends. And there's benefits. You might even work suppers when school starts. I told Mr. Fielding you'd talk to him about it."

"Oh, Mom!"

"Mental hospitals are not like you think, Jeremy. This is a chance to find out. You wanted to know how it was for Tyler."

He started out of the kitchen. "I didn't say I wanted to *work* there. Why can't you leave my work to me?"

(56)

"Just talk to him, Jeremy. Eleven-thirty at the cafeteria. You're off tomorrow, right? Jeremy, he'll be expecting you, hear?"

It was still dark when Jeremy's alarm clock went off the next morning. He grabbed it quickly and pushed in the button, then lay there listening to the silence. No one stirred in the next room. Quietly, he pulled on his jeans and shirt, stuffed some wadded-up bills into his pocket and slipped out the window.

As he walked along the street toward the beach, he saw the first fingers of light reaching up from beneath the ocean. He wondered if Gina would be able to get away so easily. In a motel, it might be hard. What if she shared a room with her folks?

But when he reached the beach, he saw a girl sitting alone and he dropped onto the sand and ran to her.

"How come everybody's sleeping through this?" she asked, watching the rising sun shimmering across the water.

He gazed out at the ocean. No matter how many times you see it, he thought, the ocean is always a spellbinder. Like it was the flute player and he was the snake rising and dancing upward out of his basket. If he kept watching, he'd soon be helpless. Maybe Tyler . . . "You hungry?" he asked aloud.

"Not really. Let's walk a bit."

"Okay." He reached down and helped her up and they walked along, hand in hand. The ocean breeze was chilling. Gina moved closer to him and he put his arm around her. "How were the historical spots?"

She shook her head with disgust. "Terrible. My mom

(57)

wanted to drive around and see all the old plantations and Dad wanted to drive down to Kitty Hawk."

"So what did you do?"

"They just argued. We went to one ratty old mansion and a tourist center where they had displays about the Wright Brothers. Then we went out to eat and they both sulked and picked through dinner."

Jeremy shook his head sympathetically.

"I don't know why they take me on these things," Gina went on. "They're supposed to be deciding and instead Dad's telling me how interesting the history of flight is and Mom is raving about life before the Civil War."

"Deciding what?"

She drew up her shoulders and let them fall. "Whether to stay together or not. That's what this 'vacation' is all about. To see if they can work things out or should get a divorce."

Jeremy drew her closer. Light was now breaking all over the ocean, with bands of pink and yellow across the sky. Only to the west was there still the soft gray of pre-dawn.

"Come on," said Jeremy. "I'll buy you breakfast."

The Pier Restaurant was a shabby little clapboard room with pinball machines in one corner and a bin full of live worms in the other. There were five tables, covered with plaid plastic tablecloths. At the counter, fishing tackle could be ordered along with breakfast. A fisherman ordered egg sandwiches to go and eyed Jeremy and Gina suspiciously. Waiting for him to leave, Jeremy took Gina to the window to watch the sea gulls hovering above the water and diving for fish.

(58)

They ordered their breakfast from the counterwoman and took it to a table by the window.

"So what do you do in Maryland when you're not baby-sitting your folks?" Jeremy asked, dousing his pancakes in syrup.

Gina was breaking little bits off her bacon strips and popping them into her mouth one at a time. "Oh, nothing special," she said. "I'm a cheerleader, so I keep pretty busy when school's on."

"No fooling? A cheerleader?"

She looked at him in mock anger. "What's the matter? I don't look like a cheerleader to you?"

"Oh, yeah. I guess you do. I just never thought about it." He put a forkful of pancakes into his mouth. It wasn't that Gina didn't look like a cheerleader. It was more that he never pictured himself being with one. The ones at school had certainly never given him a second glance.

"What about you? I bet you play football."

"Nah. I really don't go for it much." He and Gina were worlds apart. However people got divided up during the school year, summertime seemed to restore equality. Maybe it was the magic of the beach. He pictured himself slouched at his desk in a dull classroom, his mind roaming the beaches, while cheerleaders chittered like little birds and football players grunted and tackled on the cold, hard field. He wondered if Gina would still like him if they went to school together.

But their worlds were the same in one way—they both had big problems at home. Gina didn't talk about it much more than he did, but it was probably eating at her the same way. Maybe people with problems recognized each other somehow, without words, and drew together magnetically, to find strength. Thinking of that took the edge off his loneliness.

After breakfast they walked slowly down the beach, talking and picking up shells. He sat down once and played a lively little tune on his harmonica. Gina watched him, tapping her foot in time. Then he slid into a slow, moody piece, closing his eyes as he played.

"Oh, Jeremy, that's so sad!" Gina protested, getting up. She laid a hand on his shoulder. "Come on, I've got to get to work."

"Who invented work, anyway?"

She laughed. "I don't know. Bad idea, though, wasn't it?"

"Yeah, especially since I'm off today."

"Oh, bum luck!"

After seeing Gina to the Taffy Shoppe, he sat down on one of the boardwalk benches facing the ocean. A free day was not so inviting now without Gina to share it. He thought of the appointment Mom had made for him with Mr. Fielding. He supposed he should do something about it—at least call the guy and cancel.

Mom would really be on his back though, if he didn't at least talk to him. He could come up with some reason for not taking the job. It would be something to do today, anyway.

The bus let him off right at the entrance to the hospital grounds. Seaside was a collection of little square buildings on a flat, barren patch of land. He had been on the grounds when he and his father had occasionally driven his mother to work, but walking through gave him an uneasy feeling. It was strangely quiet. Very few people were outside. Had Tyler walked roads like these, longing for the sand and surf under his bare feet? Had he listened to this silence, wishing for the night sounds on the boardwalk? Or had they kept him locked up in a building all the time? Jeremy followed the signs to the cafeteria.

Mr. Fielding shook his hand and ushered him into the little office beside the serving line. From the office window, Jeremy could see workers lining up little dishes of pudding on the glass shelves. Mom had mentioned something about patients working there. He wondered which ones they were.

"I was anxious to talk with you, Jeremy. Your mother hasn't worked in the cafeteria, of course, but she has a good reputation here. Always on time, very few sick days. Been here a good many years, too, hasn't she?"

"Yes, sir. I guess so."

"Well, when she said her boy was looking for work, I was hoping you might be our man."

"Do you have patients working here?"

"Yes, a few. But there's nothing to be afraid of. They get looked over better than anyone you'd work with on the outside before they get work clearance."

"Oh, I'm not afraid," Jeremy said. "I just wondered."

"Well, we use a few patients, but we like to balance them with some outside people. The patients aren't usually as stable, and it's good for them to work with others. Also, they usually go home before too long." He tapped his pencil on the desk. "Your mother says you might be able to stay on in the school year."

"Well, I'm not sure. You see, I have a job—"

"Oh." Mr. Fielding looked disappointed. "Your mother said you were interested in mental hospitals. This is a good way to—"

"Mr. Fielding." One of the cafeteria women appeared in the doorway. "Lucy's saying she wants to go back to her ward. I can't do a thing with her. Can you come talk to her?"

"Yes. Excuse me a minute, Jeremy," he said, getting up.

The moment alone gave Jeremy a chance to think things over. He *had* been wondering what Tyler had gone through at the hospital, been haunted by it. Now here was his chance to find out. So what if he liked Hot Dog Alley better? Tyler had liked being free better, but did he get to choose? And what was so great about a hot dog joint, anyway? He had *said* he wanted to find answers. . . .

Mr. Fielding strode back into the room. "Jeremy, I'm sorry. Little interruptions. I didn't realize you already had a job—"

"It's not a great job, sir. I was thinking of quitting."

"Well, we're just minimum wage here. Of course, there are benefits. You'll have to decide what's best for you."

"When would you like me to start, sir?"

"I know you'll need to give notice—"

"I can tell him today and start tomorrow, if you'd like."

Mr. Fielding smiled. "If you could, that would help us a great deal. We're rather shorthanded."

"All right," said Jeremy, standing up. "I'll be here at seven o'clock tomorrow morning."

5

While telling Jim he was quitting at Hot Dog Alley, Jeremy had not felt so sure of his decision. Jim was disappointed.

"I thought you liked this job, Jeremy," he said. "You were doing real well."

"I do like it. But there's this other job at Seaside Hospital—"

"Oh, they pay better, huh?"

"No. . . ."

"You'd rather be cooped up in a mental hospital in the summertime?"

"It's a personal thing. It's hard to explain."

It was hard to explain to Gina, too. He hadn't even thought of her when he accepted the new job.

"Oh, well, I guess I won't be seeing much of you," Gina had said.

"Sure you will. I still get off at three and it's only a fifteen-minute bus ride."

"Yeah, but it's not like working next door."

Now, rattling along on the bus in the early morning, Jeremy stole a glance at his mother. Her forehead was creased as if she were struggling with her thoughts. Finally, she pulled her purse up on her lap and laid her hands across the clasp. "Jeremy, I'm real glad you took this job. That was smart."

"Well, I wanted to check the place out, like you said."

"Yes. You'll see it's a good place. Clean. Lots of doctors and programs. It's not the hospital that has to answer for Tyler." She paused as the bus stopped to pick up passengers and then lurched forward again. "You know, there's only so much a mother can do for a son. Comes a time a man needs to step in. There's ways men have with each other. Delbert never could talk to Tyler, though."

Jeremy looked at her in surprise. "You blame Pop for Tyler?"

"No," she said hurriedly. "It just might have helped if they could talk. Jeremy, my father was a drunk and died when I was twelve. My mother fell all apart then—for some reason, she loved the guy. I had to 'bout raise myself. There's not a whole lot to be proud of in this family, Jeremy. Father never fought whiskey. Mother never fought anything. Tyler was like them. He never fought the weakness in his mind. That's what I blame." Her eyes had become dark, narrow lines. "Someday you'll be called on to fight. Will you do it, or will you throw up your hands?"

He did not answer. He wasn't sure there was an answer. It seemed to him that you didn't get an invitation to battle. Rather, your own particular trouble came, knocked you off your feet and dragged you away. If you were lucky, you survived it. Was there really any other way?

They parted company at the entrance, Mom heading for C Ward where she worked and Jeremy for the cafeteria.

The cafeteria was a hive of activity when Jeremy walked in.

"I'm afraid you're going to have to jump into things all at once, Jeremy," Mr. Fielding said. "The smoke'll clear a little between breakfast and lunch." He grabbed the arm of a tall, blond young man in his late teens. "Donnie, this is Jeremy. He'll be your new partner on rounds. Jeremy, Donnie. He'll show you everything."

"You can help load up the food cart," said Donnie. "Grab trays from the belt. Make sure the tags say A Ward and then slide 'em like this."

Jeremy fell into the work and when they had loaded two carts, the second for B Ward, he and Donnie pushed them out of the cafeteria building and headed for the wards.

"What kind of place is A Ward?" Jeremy asked.

"Admissions. They stick everybody there at first 'til they figure out what to do with 'em. You're not from here, are you?"

"Sure. I was born in Baxter. Been here all my life. Just haven't been around the hospital."

"That's what I meant."

Now they stood at the doorway of A Ward where Tyler

must have stood the day he went in. Donnie pressed the buzzer for the door to be unlocked from within.

"Sometimes it takes a minute if they're busy," he said.

Maybe they were busy the day Tyler came, and left him standing there like a beggar at the door, Jeremy thought. The two police officers on either side of him shifting their weight from one leg to another, impatient to be done with him and go on their lunch break. And Tyler, alone in the world, willing himself back to his bedroom hideaway where he could close his eyes on the world. Hungering for a cigarette and the strength to face what lay beyond the locked door.

Jeremy felt a fluttering in his own stomach just at the thought that the building was full of crazy people. Then a nurse appeared behind the screened window and the door was opened.

"You boys are a little late, aren't you?" she said.

"New guy," said Donnie.

The door was locked behind them and Jeremy stood there awkwardly, surveying the ward. He had expected to find himself in the midst of pandemonium, a regular snake pit, but the ward was quiet. No people screaming or writhing on the floor. A hall stretched out before them in either direction and nearby a couple of young guys stood talking and smoking cigarettes. They must have been patients, Jeremy figured, or they wouldn't have had the time to hang out that way. But they didn't have on pajamas. They looked like regular guys.

In front of them was an open room with several couches, little tables and a TV set. The breeze blew gently in through the heavy screens on the windows and ruffled the thin blue curtains.

"Come on, Jeremy," said Donnie, pushing his cart down the hall.

Jeremy followed him into the dining hall, where they unloaded the trays, calling out the names and delivering them to the tables. A couple of times no one would answer and the nurse showed them who the tray belonged to.

When Donnie's cart was empty, they took Jeremy's to B Ward and then headed back to the cafeteria.

"You been working here long?" asked Jeremy.

"Couple weeks."

"Like it?"

"Oh, yeah, it's the bee's knees," said Donnie sarcastically. He nudged his cart over a hump in the walkway with his foot. "I guess it beats hanging out, talking to the crazies. See, I'm *from* here. I mean from *here,*" he emphasized, pointing to the ground. "And I would like to be gone from here, but I can't yet. Understand?"

"Yeah."

Back at the cafeteria, Donnie carried a breakfast tray over to a seat by the window and Mr. Fielding started Jeremy on sorting the silverware as it came out of the dishwasher.

"Donnie done for today?"

"Yes," said Mr. Fielding. "The job is only one part of the patient's program. Did everything go all right?"

"Yes, sir. Fine."

The next day Jeremy met Donnie coming up the walk to the cafeteria.

"You back again?" asked Donnie.

"Yeah, I thought I would come. You didn't think I would?"

"I thought maybe all the crazies would give you the willies—send you running for the hills."

Jeremy looked at him squarely. "Do I look that jumpy to you?"

Donnie met his look and then grinned. "No." He clapped Jeremy on the back. "Come on, there's a hundred rumbling stomachs in A and B Wards!"

Jeremy grinned back and trotted after him into the building.

As they were pushing their loaded carts toward the wards, Donnie asked, "What are you doing here, anyway?"

"I need a job," Jeremy said simply.

"Yeah, but why *here*?"

Jeremy hesitated. "I had a brother here for a while."

"Yeah? How long's he been out?"

"He's dead." Instantly he regretted saying it. It was a dumb thing to tell a patient who was trying to get out himself. He glanced at Donnie's grave face. "He was pretty sick," Jeremy added quickly. "Schizophrenic."

"Aw, these jerks," said Donnie angrily. "They don't know what's wrong with anyone! They don't know what to do!" He fell silent for a while. "You want to see what this place is like?"

"Yeah, that's why—"

"Look, I've got free time at three today. I'll show you around, if you want."

"Yeah, I do."

Donnie was waiting for him when he got off work. First he took him to the activities building. There were classrooms for woodworking, leather-crafting, ceramics, academic subjects, and even job skills.

"I got my General Education Degree here," said Donnie.

"Really? I didn't know you could go to school at a hospital."

"Sure. They might send me to barber school when I get out. I got a counselor working on it."

"Where?"

"Well, there's one in Elizabeth City and a little dinky one in Baxter Beach. I hope I get the one in Baxter—I'd sure like to hang out at the beach a while after being cooped up here so long."

"Yeah, and if I ever feel like I need a haircut, you could do it."

Donnie smiled. "This is the Medical Ward. It's mostly for old people, but also for people who overdose and things like that."

There wasn't a lot to see there—an empty hallway with rooms of two beds each. Jeremy didn't want to stare into the rooms and meet the eyes of the people lying there. From a couple of rooms he heard soft moaning or talking. He noticed the floors were clean—shining, even.

"Now, you want to see my ward?"

"Sure. What kind of ward is it?"

"D is open men's. That means they don't lock you up, you can come and go. It's for guys almost ready to leave."

D Ward was like the others Jeremy had seen, except

that there was no waiting at the door. Donnie's room was a little cubicle with two desk-wardrobe units and two beds. There was a painting on the wall. It was an ordinary beach scene, the type you'd buy frame and all in the dime store.

"I'd shut the door but if I did the aide would only come down and hassle us. They don't really trust you, even here."

"But you know, I thought the place would look a lot worse. What do you really think of this place?"

It took Donnie a minute to answer. "Jeremy, do you like school?"

"Not really."

"Are you learning anything there?"

"I suppose I am, even when I don't like it."

"Well, that's about how it is, only school starts to look good by comparison."

"But you said the doctors didn't know what they were doing."

"I get mad when they mess up on somebody like your brother. And they do that—walk around in their ties with their degrees and these poor suckers here can't even get through the day. Listen, there's doctors here that'll write you up for 'laughing inappropriately'—I mean *laughing*, man! Just 'cause they don't see the joke, they call us crazy! But there are a few doctors who care."

"Do they ever lock people up in rooms by themselves?"

"Come on," said Donnie. "They call it time-out." He showed Jeremy a locked room down the hall. Jeremy looked through the little window in the door. It was

empty, except for a mattress on the floor. The walls were padded.

"Why do they have this in D Ward?"

"Not everybody goes home from here. Sometimes they go back to the locked ward."

"But why do they need this room?"

"Guys break bad. Last week this guy we call Bobcat went tearing through here like a wild man, rattling heads."

"Why didn't they talk to him, try to calm him down?"

"Shoot!" Donnie laughed. "You couldn't have talked to Bobcat!"

"Jeremy looked into the room again. The hair prickled on the back of his neck. He wondered how many hours Tyler had spent screaming and crying in a little hole like this. "How long do they keep guys here?"

"Not long by the clock, I guess. Just seems long." He walked down the hall, stopping to light a cigarette from the lighter chained to the nurse's station wall. "Look, I'll see you Monday. I got stuff to do now."

On Saturday he met Gina at the beach and they decided to go into town to the bowling alley. The bus dropped them off in the center of town, a short distance from the alley. On the way Jeremy stopped at the sports shop and looked in the window. "I'm saving up for diving gear," he said.

"Do you skin-dive?"

"I never have," he admitted. "Haven't had the gear, but I've always wanted to."

"To hunt for treasure chests and stuff?"

"Well, maybe. But mostly to learn about the ocean. I want to be an oceanographer." The word rolled off his tongue so comfortably now. Each time he said it, it seemed closer—a real possibility.

"You wouldn't catch me down there with those sharks," said Gina.

"I'll bet you'd love it, Gina. Did you know it's not all just flat under there? There's mountains and canyons and plains just like on land. And scientists have learned that the seafloor is actually younger than the continents. Studying the ocean might tell us about the history of man."

Gina shook her head. "Seems to me we pick everything apart too much. We study a thing every which way until there's no beauty left. You can't see the whole of it."

Jeremy's thoughts shifted suddenly. If he had been able to study what was happening to Tyler, instead of focusing on the whole, maybe he could have understood. "Maybe if people were willing to pick things apart, they wouldn't make so many mistakes," he said aloud.

"You sound like my mother trying to get my father to go to a marriage counselor."

"What does he say?"

"He says, 'You go right ahead, Marian. Let me know how it works out.' He hates all that psychological stuff."

"Are they doing any better?"

She shook her head. "Last night they made a big deal about going out dancing, and then they came in at ten-thirty, all steamed up about something."

"Do you think they're going to stay here much longer?"

(72)

"I hope so," Gina said vehemently. "I don't want to leave."

Jeremy gave her hand a squeeze and they started walking again.

"Dad started talking about going back home, but Mom said that would be 'breaking their commitment'—whatever that was."

"Well, whatever it was, I hope she wins."

The bowling alley door was wedged in between a drugstore and a real estate office. Jeremy pulled open the door and they descended the narrow steps to the alley below. There was only one other lane in use. The place was usually deserted in the summer, unless it rained. They bowled two games and then went to the empty snack area for hamburgers and shakes.

"I miss you at work. There's a new girl at Hot Dog Alley and she is dull, dull, dull. How do you like the new job?"

"I like it. The work is nothing great, but I was wondering what it's like at a mental hospital."

"And?"

"Well, it's not bad. Once I thought it would be awful. But they keep it up pretty nice and they have lots of things for patients to do. In fact, I'm working with a patient—a guy named Donnie."

"What's he like?"

"A little hard to know at first. But we're getting to be friends. I don't know why he's there. He's sure not crazy."

"Maybe he's just getting well again."

"Maybe. But I think a lot of people end up in those places who shouldn't have. Donnie got his G.E.D. at the hospital and they're going to send him to barber school—maybe right here in Baxter Beach."

"I'm glad *somebody's* story is having a happy ending." Gina finished off her milk shake. "Come on, let's go back to the beach."

"Okay," said Jeremy, getting up. "You know, I really hope Donnie comes to the beach when he gets out. I could help him get started with things. It might help to have a friend here."

It was too late to help Tyler, but there was Donnie and it was not too late for him.

6

On Sunday Gina had to go somewhere with her parents again. Mom and Pop dressed themselves up to go see some former neighbors who had moved to Elizabeth City.

"George opened his own dry-cleaning place," Mom told Jeremy as she stood pinning up her hair in front of the mirror.

"Yeah? How's it going?"

"Very well. He's an ambitious man and Millie helps him run the place." She patted her hair down and studied it. "I'm hoping they'll be an influence on Delbert."

"How's that?"

She glanced out the bedroom door. "Where's your father?"

"Out messing with the car."

"I been setting aside money, Jeremy," she said in a low voice, "for your father to open his own business."

"Does Pop want to do that?"

"Every man wants to be his own boss, honey. I think once he kinda hoped you boys'd follow him—Delbert Chase & Sons, Custodial Services. But ain't no reason it couldn't be just his. I'm hoping he'll see how good George's doing and want to move, too."

"You mean to Elizabeth City? Leave the beach?"

"Why, yes, Jeremy. There's no opportunity here. Be nice to get away from all this grit and sand and get a nice apartment in the city."

Jeremy had a sudden sinking sensation. He hoped Pop wouldn't go for the idea. "Do you have enough money saved for all this?"

"No," she said. "Not near enough. I just want your father to start thinking on it."

The screen door banged shut and they heard Pop come in. "Shh!" warned Mom. "Don't let your father know none of this!"

After they had left Jeremy went out to the backyard. Mom could make it in an apartment okay, he thought. She never used the yard except to hang the laundry. None of them used it anymore really. Pop only walked through it to the shed where his tools were kept. The old picnic table was grimy from lack of attention. The tire swing was dangling from the one tree like an old black doughnut. Why had no one bothered to take it down in all these years?

Maybe if he could fix the yard up, Mom would have

second thoughts about leaving. He cut down the tire and stored it under the house. Then he got a bowl of hot soapy water and started scrubbing the picnic table. He could suggest dinner out there one evening. But there ought to be an outside light in case they sat out late. Mom hated sitting in the dark. And he could say, "Why not invite George and Millie Henley over here this time? I bet they miss Baxter, all cooped up in the city with no yard. We could hang paper lanterns all around and have a yard party."

He unlocked the shed. Up on the shelf was the globe kitchen light that Pop had taken down when he put in the new fixture. It would look a little weird as a yard light, but it would do. He gathered up the screwdriver, drill and electrical wire and headed into the house.

He'd never worked with electricity, but he'd seen Tyler put a new plug in their room once. It wasn't dangerous, so long as you remembered to cut the current by unscrewing the fuse.

There was an outlet on the kitchen wall that he could draw current from. He removed the plate, attached the wire and then drilled through to the outside. Next he attached the light to the house and connected the wire to it. Screw the fuse in, and—he ran back out to see it. There it was, big and bright as the moon, pinned to the side of their house. It would look great at night!

There was only one problem. How to turn it off. He'd forgotten about a switch! They could just unscrew the light bulb, but it would be a pain taking that glass globe off and on, and if they kept the fuse out, it would cut off some electricity within the house.

He rummaged around the shed for a socket with a chain, but there was none. Good time to get out for a walk, anyway. He gathered up the tools, put them in the shed, unscrewed the light bulb and replaced the globe.

There was a little hardware store open on Sundays down at the corner of Ocean Avenue and Fulton, at the south end of the beach. He liked walking down there anyway. It was where the town was petering out, mostly ramshackle old houses and a few stores. The beach itself was nearly deserted there.

As Jeremy came out of the hardware store with the chain socket, he noticed a young woman standing at the top of the stairs in a building across the street. She was shaking out a rug. She wore an ankle-length skirt and a peasant blouse. Her long dark hair was gathered into a thick braid at her back.

"Angela?" he called tentatively.

She turned. "Jeremy!" She laid the rug over the railing and started down the stairs.

He ran to hug her.

"Oh, it's *so* good to see you!" she cried.

"I thought you moved to Sunland."

"I did. I'm just moving back here now. Todd—that's my guy—he just got a job. Well, come on up, can you? We have so much to catch up on!"

"Sure I can."

He followed her up the stairs. Her guy, Jeremy thought in surprise. He'd never given much thought to Angela and guys. She'd been out some, of course, but nothing serious. From Jeremy's vantage point, she'd always seemed aloof from all that. But maybe she had just kept her relationships private.

The little apartment was strewn with boxes waiting to be unpacked. "Whew!" said Jeremy. "You have more plants than ever!"

"Yeah!" Angela laughed. "They really make the air nice, you know. Lost some of them in the move, though."

"When did you get back?"

"Just two days ago."

"You want some help unpacking?"

"What I want is a good excuse to take a break—I'm exhausted! You want some ice tea? I've got a pitcherful in the fridge."

"Sounds good. So tell me about Todd."

"Todd." She handed him a tall glass of ice tea. "Well, Todd is a construction worker. He just got a job at that new motel going up by the interstate, so that's why we moved. We met in Sunland and started seeing each other. Come on, let's sit down. He moved in, which was a good thing. I was having trouble making the rent. I was selling plants on the boardwalk."

"That's good—that he could help you, I mean. Is he nice? Do you get along?"

"Oh, yes," she said hurriedly. "I didn't mean to make it sound that way—we've gotten close. He's—a strong person."

That made sense, Jeremy thought. Angela was always after Pop for being a weakling—not speaking up for himself or taking a stand. Seemed like she'd do things just to try to make him angry. But then, on those rare occasions when he tried to get firm with her, she'd put him down for it. She'd have to pick a guy who was strong.

"But let's talk about you." She tucked her feet under her and settled back into the worn old couch. "You got a girl friend?"

"Sort of. There's this girl, Gina."

"Summer girl?"

"Unfortunately. Her folks came here to decide if they should divorce."

Angela shook her head. "Everybody's got family problems! Makes me wonder if it's possible for that whole family scene to work out." She tipped her head, gazing at Jeremy. "You sure have grown. I can't get over it, how you look like—"

"—Tyler," Jeremy finished with a grimace.

"Yeah, Tyler. Sore subject, huh?"

"Sore because I hear it all the time. I look like Tyler, act like Tyler, think like Tyler. Whatever happened to Jeremy?"

"I'm sorry, Jer, I didn't mean all that."

"I know. It's okay. I know I look like Tyler. I just get buggy because it seems like Mom is never seeing *me*."

"Nothing's changed at home, has it?" Angela picked up one of the black-velvet pillows. The moon and stars were embroidered on it in silver thread. "Remember these?"

"Yeah. You made 'em for Mom."

"Right, but I took them back because she never did care about them."

"I remember she said pillows should be plain or plaid, maybe, but those looked like something to hang on the wall. Funny."

"Not to me," Angela answered vehemently. "No matter what you do, what you are, she'll run you down for it. You'll *never* find yourself in that place, Jeremy." She laid the pillow down and settled back against the couch.

"Things have never been right since Tyler drowned. She keeps thinking I might go crazy, too. So she nags me a lot."

"And Pop doesn't say a word."

"Not much."

"Jeremy, they've *always* been that way. It's nothing new. How do you think Tyler got crazy?"

Jeremy didn't answer. Did Mom yell Tyler into craziness and Pop ignore him into it? Did he go to sleep normal one night and wake up to find the world turned inside out? Or was it a refuge he slipped off to sideways, when no one was looking. A place of power, where he could set things right. Only he couldn't and so he had to die. . . .

"You ought to get out of there," Angela continued. "For your own sake."

"That's what I say some days," Jeremy joked. "Lemme outa this place!"

Angela dismissed his humor with a shake of her head. "No, I mean it, Jeremy. It's not healthy there. Tyler showed us that."

"Look, I'll admit it gets rough at home sometimes, but at fifteen, where am I going to go?"

"Maybe—maybe you could stay here. Sure, that'd be a good idea."

Jeremy smiled. "Thanks, Ange, but I couldn't do that."

"Why not?"

"What about Todd?"

"It'd be good for him. Besides, it's my place, too, and if a sister can't help out her kid brother . . ."

A gust of ocean wind blew in the open window and the little lilies of the valley in their earthen pot bobbed their heads.

"I—I don't know, Angela," said Jeremy uncertainly. "This is all coming up kind of suddenly."

"Well, you think about it. You know, I am dying for a peach. You want to go to the grocery with me? I need to pick up some things anyway."

They descended the stairs and fell in step together, Angela's long skirt swishing around her ankles as she walked. She fingered her braid. "It's so good to be with you again, Jeremy. I know I didn't used to feel this way, but things are changing for me. Family's important."

"Seems like our family's split up every which way now. Mom and Pop—it's like there's something between them now. They both seem to blame each other for Tyler."

"Well, they ought to," Angela said flatly.

"I don't know. Sometimes I've blamed myself."

"You!"

"Yeah. For not understanding what was happening."

"Look, you were a kid. That was Mom and Pop's department, but they don't know a nickel's worth about raising kids. They'd have been better off raising potatoes!"

The grocery door swung open in front of them and they left the damp heat for the cool of the store. The hairs stood up on Jeremy's arms.

(82)

Angela wrestled one cart free from the others. "I wasn't talking about Mom and Pop when I said family's important. I mean, what can you do with them? But you and I are family, right, Jeremy?"

"Sure, we're family."

They walked slowly down the aisles as Angela selected her food.

"I think I'll get some potting soil," Angela was saying.

"Are you going to sell plants here, too?"

"Maybe." Angela's eyes moved quickly over the directions on the bag of soil, but her thoughts appeared to be elsewhere. "Jeremy, don't tell Mom or Pop, but I'm going to have a baby."

"What?"

A woman peered over at them suddenly and Angela pushed the cart away. "God, I hope she realizes you're my little brother! Todd's baby. You heard me."

"Wow. I don't know what to say."

"Congratulations? Best wishes?" She smiled uncertainly. "You'll be an uncle."

"Yeah."

Taking the groceries through the checkout line gave Jeremy a little time to try to collect his thoughts. He supposed he should be happy for her—it was a new life and all that. Something to distract them from the specter of death. But the way she announced it—her eyes riveted to the bag of potting soil—and the quiver in her smile, bothered him. And then there was the picture she painted of Todd—a macho construction worker who helped with the rent. It didn't have the makings of a happy home. No wonder she was talking family suddenly.

Jeremy picked up the bag of groceries and they headed back to the apartment. "Mom and Pop will be grandparents," he commented.

She shrugged. "Technically. But don't tell them, Jeremy. All I need is Mom over here ranting and raving about how I botched it up again and brought shame to the family. And then telling me how to raise him like she's an expert."

"But they're bound to see you sometime. Baxter's not all that big."

"Then it can't be helped. But at least I'll have had a few more months of peace. They probably won't care anyway. There's no love lost between them and me. You know that."

"Are you going to get married?"

"Well, Todd's not exactly a settling-down kind of man, you know what I mean? But maybe when he sees the baby . . . when he holds him . . . I think it might change."

Angela unlocked the apartment door and Jeremy set the bag down on the kitchen table.

"Ange, I think you're being too tough on Mom and Pop. I know they bungle things up a lot, but they really do care."

Angela didn't answer.

"And like you said, family's important. Especially with that baby coming. I'm just one part of your family. Mom and Pop could help you."

"Jeremy, they didn't even try to find me that whole year in Sunland!"

"You told them not to!"

"I know . . ."

She turned away, but Jeremy caught the disappointment in her eyes, the wistfulness in her voice. She had wanted them to come after her. To insist she come home. But she was grown—a woman! How could you ever figure out what people needed? Like Tyler, needing one thing and straining with all his might toward another.

Donnie was not in the cafeteria on Monday morning. Jeremy had just begun loading the food carts when Mr. Fielding came up with someone new. "Jeremy, this is Bill. He'll be your new partner."

"Where's Donnie?"

"Uh, Bill, start loading the carts, will you? I want to have a word with Jeremy."

Mr. Fielding put a hand on Jeremy's shoulder and guided him away from the other workers. "Bill's been here before, so he knows what he's doing. You won't have to break him in really—maybe just keep him on the track from time to time."

"Yeah. But where's Donnie?"

"Jeremy, Donnie did some backsliding this weekend. He's in the Medical Ward."

"What happened?"

"Overdose."

"On purpose? He was trying to kill himself?"

"I'm afraid so."

"But why?"

Mr. Fielding shrugged. "Who knows, Jeremy? Who can ever really know?"

Jeremy stared at him a moment and then walked numbly back to the work area and began loading the carts. It didn't make sense! Donnie was okay—a regular guy. But then there was the way he had abruptly left Jeremy when they were talking about the time-out room. . . . He had other things to do, that was all. Maybe that talk about Tyler . . .

The last tray was loaded and he and Bill began pushing the carts to A Ward. By the time they had distributed the trays there, Jeremy could stand it no longer. He pushed his empty cart beside the building.

"Look, Bill, cover for me on B, will you?" he said. "There's something I gotta do."

"Oh, sure man, sure man. That's neat. You just go and do any little old thing you want."

"I'll make it up to you, Bill, honest," promised Jeremy, breaking into a run. "I'll be back real soon."

"Oh, right. Good old Bill just loves to do his own work and everybody else's, too. Hey, J, can I shine your shoes for you, too?"

When Jeremy reached the Medical Ward he drew in his breath sharply, trying to slow his pounding heart. He'd have to be calm, to say the right things. Maybe Donnie would be talking crazy, like Tyler. But that stuff wasn't new to him; he wouldn't let it throw him. He knew the real Donnie—well, a little bit, anyhow. He would talk to that Donnie. Like a brother.

He found Donnie's room and slipped into it unnoticed. Donnie lay motionless and white beneath the crisp sheets. His breakfast tray of juice, broth and gelatin sat untouched on the table.

He touched Donnie's shoulder. "Hey, buddy, aren't you going to eat that gourmet breakfast?"

Donnie's eyes opened slowly. "What do you want?"

"Just came to see how you were doing."

"Well, now you've seen, so you can be on your merry way."

Jeremy sat down on the arm of the chair beside the bed. "No kidding, how are you doing?"

Donnie sighed and looked away.

"Why don't you get it off your chest, Donnie?"

"Why don't you get out—what are you, a shrink now?"

Jeremy stood up, wavering. It wasn't coming out right. But why? He was blowing it all over again, just like with Tyler. "Donnie, what happened?" he burst out. "Why are you doing this? You were gonna get out, go to school, live at the beach! What's wrong?"

Donnie sat up suddenly, waving his arms. The IV tube drew tight, twisting the needle that went into the back of his hand. "Get out of here! Get out! Get out!" he screamed.

Suddenly a nurse appeared. "Young man, what are you doing here? Donnie isn't to have visitors yet. Here, Donnie, lie down, let me fix that IV." She leaned over Donnie and looked back at Jeremy. "Go on now, before you make matters worse."

Jeremy staggered backward out of the room and fled the building. He sank down against the wall outside and put his head in his hands. Make matters worse, that was all he *had* done. But why? He felt totally drained, as if he could sit against that building, still as a rock and never move again.

After a while, he lifted his head. He thought of Bill and

pulled himself to his feet and headed slowly toward B Ward. The cart he had left there was gone, so he turned toward the cafeteria, walking more quickly now.

Bill was finishing up his breakfast when Jeremy came in and Mr. Fielding had evidently been waiting for him as he met him at the door.

"Jeremy, come into my office, please," he said, closing the door behind him. He sat down and folded his hands. "Sit down. Jeremy, Bill came back alone with two carts this morning."

"Yes, sir. I didn't mean to be gone so long. I'm sorry."

"Jeremy, you shouldn't have been gone at all. It wasn't fair to Bill. Or to the patients in the wards who are expecting their meals at a certain time. When a meal's delayed, it can throw off program schedules throughout the day. More important is the message you gave Bill. One of the reasons we hire outside help is to have role models for our patients. Do you know what I mean by that?"

Jeremy shook his head.

"To act as an example. For a person like Bill, who's in and out of here as if there were a revolving door, that's crucial. He needs an example of stability from within his peer group—"

"Mr. Fielding, I'm sorry. I was upset about Donnie. I went to see him."

Mr. Fielding nodded. "I'm afraid setbacks like that are something you'll have to become accustomed to, Jeremy."

"But why, Mr. Fielding? He was on D Ward, getting ready to go out. He was going to go to barber school. He hated it here. Why would he ruin it all?"

"It's hard to understand. Part of him wanted to leave, true, but another part was apparently very frightened and so he sabotaged his own plans. It's not uncommon."

"Then why do the doctors try to send them home?"

"Unfortunately, often the doctors don't pick it up. They don't always know what to do to help a patient either. Sometimes they believe a person's okay and ready to go when it's really too soon."

Jeremy looked out the office window at a woman setting up desserts on the cafeteria line. He felt a heavy sadness. Mr. Fielding was saying that the doctors, despite all their learning, might not have an answer for Donnie. Perhaps there hadn't been one for Tyler either.

"You're finding this is not an ordinary cafeteria job. There are a lot of hard lessons here." Mr. Fielding stood up. "Well, time moves on. Before long it'll be time to take the lunch trays out."

At lunchtime Mr. Fielding asked Jeremy to deliver the D Ward trays himself.

Maybe it'll be good, Jeremy thought as he pushed the cart down the pathway, to get in D and see some guys who have it together. Guys who are going to make it.

When he went into the dining hall, Bill was sitting tilted back in a chair with his feet up on the radiator. He swung his legs down and stood up when he saw Jeremy. "Well, delivering food these days, are we?"

"Look, Bill, I'm sorry I stuck you with all that this morning—I was just shook up about something."

"Shook up about Donnie-boy?" Bill grinned. "Mustn't get attached to the patients, J, they're far too unreliable."

Jeremy turned away to open up the cart, but Bill lopped an arm over the top and looked into his face. "We all knew old pill-eater wouldn't make it—just a matter of time. Doesn't have any guts whatsoever."

"Shut up, Bill."

"Shut up, Bill," Bill mimicked. He turned to the others seated around them. "I do believe this here outside boy is getting upset. Quick, get the tranquilizers, lock him up quick, quick!"

Without thinking, Jeremy lunged for him, grabbing him by the shirt. Somebody hollered. The room was buzzing with noise and Jeremy felt himself grabbed from behind and pulled away.

When the man loosened his hold, Jeremy found himself in the hall, looking at an aide, while a nurse urged the patients back into the dining hall.

"Jeez, man!" exclaimed the aide. "Why'd you let that guy get to you that way? Man, they'll set you up, get you swinging and you'll be in court so fast—"

The nurse stomped over. "Young man, I want you to report to Mr. Fielding immediately."

"Uh, the cart—"

"You never mind about the cart. We'll send it up. You just get yourself into his office pronto. I'll be calling as you go!"

Mr. Fielding was grim when Jeremy walked in. "Jeremy, I thought we had things settled this morning."

"Sir, that guy, Bill—he really got on me. He was looking for a fight. Hassling me about Donnie—"

"—Another situation that is not uncommon."

"But what do you expect—"

"Jeremy, at Seaside we have to keep a rein on our emotions because of those around us who have no control. I can understand your feelings. You're new and this business with Donnie was a shock. But attacking a patient is a serious offense. I have no choice but to suspend you without pay for three days."

Jeremy jumped up, pulling off his apron. "Yeah, well, I can't walk around here like a zombie, like I don't care what's happening and let a guy walk all over me! So you can keep your stinking job and find yourself another 'role model'!"

He threw the apron onto Mr. Fielding's desk and stormed out.

7

He waited until the usual time before going home. Mom had the day off and would notice an early arrival. With her working at the hospital, the whole incident would come out soon enough, but at least he might buy a day or two of peace to think things over.

When he reached the house, a bed was sitting out on the curb. It was Tyler's. He ran his fingers over the wooden headboard and then went in the house.

Pop was sitting at the kitchen table sipping coffee. Mom was standing at the sink doing the dishes. She shook the suds from her hands and wiped them on the dish towel.

"How was work today, Jeremy?"

"Okay. What's Tyler's bed doing out front?"

"Goodwill's coming."

Jeremy flung open the door to his room. There was a gaping emptiness across from his bed, where Tyler's bed had been. The sight shocked him. Every night for over a year he'd lain across from that empty bed, knowing Tyler would not sleep in it again. And even though Tyler's other things had long since been taken out, the absence of the bed was wrenching.

Pop came over and put a hand on his shoulder. "Give you a little more breathing room, son," he said.

"Somebody could be using that bed," said Mom, plunging her hands into the soapy water again. "Don't know why we waited."

Jeremy looked at her and nodded. It's hard on her to get rid of it, too, he realized. Another letting-go. You don't let go of somebody you love just once. You do it over and over again, little by little. That was the hell of it.

"I'm fixing an early supper tonight," Mom said. "Pop has to go in to work this evening."

"Okay."

He went into his room, closed the door and lay down on the floor where Tyler's bed had been, staring up at the ceiling. How many nights had Tyler lain there, looking at the ceiling, feeling all kinds of terrible things, he wondered. And with his own brother sleeping away across from him not even knowing. Tears sprang up suddenly in his eyes and he slammed his fist down on the floor.

He couldn't help Tyler. He couldn't help Donnie. He couldn't even keep a job and help his parents or himself.

He closed his eyes and felt the pressure of his shoulder

blades against the floorboards. Life was such a struggle. It must have felt that way to Tyler, too. Every day.

About an hour had passed when Mom called him to dinner, awakening him. He sat up, rubbing his eyes. "Coming!" I must have been really beat to fall asleep on the hard floor, he thought.

At the stove his mother dropped a tangle of spaghetti onto his plate, and he carried it to the table.

"So how was your visit with the Henleys?" Jeremy asked.

"Fine, just fine," said Mom. "George drove us by his dry-cleaning store. Nice place, good location."

"A real headache, though," said Pop. "Doctor told Millie not to work and George can't find decent help."

"Sure, but I bet he wouldn't trade being his own boss," Mom returned.

Pop shook his head. "What's that worth, Lydia? Worrying about money coming in and going out. Me, I'd rather have a starting time and a stopping time and forget about work after that."

Jeremy caught the disappointment on Mom's face, but he couldn't help feeling relieved. She'd keep working on him, he was sure of that. But at least he didn't have to worry about a move anytime soon.

"I saw Angela yesterday," said Jeremy.

Mom stopped eating and looked at him. Pop's questioning gaze was also on him.

"She's fine," he went on. "Going to be living in Baxter now."

"What—is she doing?" Mom asked haltingly.

"Uh, well, getting along, I suppose. I helped her get groceries."

(94)

Mom nodded. Her voice was wistful. "I always had Angela figured for a real good job. Like a secretary for some big company. She was a smart girl. Had lots of energy."

The spaghetti turned to a dry lump in Jeremy's mouth. There it was again. The all-important job and the kid that didn't measure up. Tyler, the brain that flipped out. Angela, the energetic secretary that never was. And Jeremy, the jobless.

"Is she working, son?"

"Not yet, Pop. She sold plants in Sunland. Maybe she'll do that here, too. We didn't talk about that stuff much." He took a swallow of milk. "The apartment was pretty nice, though."

A little flicker of relief passed briefly over Mom's face. A nice place was a good sign. She had no doubt pictured Angela living in filth and poverty.

"There were lots of plants."

Mom smiled. "Angela always did like plants. Once I had her figured for going to college and studying biology or botany—whatever it is about plants. But she was too impatient for school. That was her flaw, she was impatient."

"Well, she seems pretty content now."

"Did—did she talk about missing us? About wanting to come home?"

"Not exactly."

"She's proud," Pop said.

"Yes, proud." Mom latched onto the word as if it held an answer. As if it was the name of a small hurdle one had only to jump over to restore the natural order of things. "She always was proud. Jeremy, do you think you could talk to her? Tell her we don't hold no grudge—she could come back."

They don't hold a grudge! thought Jeremy. Mom threatening to whack the tops off Angela's plants and *she* doesn't hold a grudge! Good lord, Angela was *twenty* when she left. But Mom's face was a slate wiped clean of all that turmoil—she was only a mother who missed her daughter.

"Maybe you ought to go see her."

Mom and Pop exchanged glances.

"She told us not to," said Pop.

"A mother shouldn't have to go chasing all over town to see her daughter," said Mom. "A daughter should come to her mother."

Jeremy looked at them—Pop, resigned; Mom, her face growing firm with her own pride. You'd think, with Tyler dead, that the rest of the family would try to come together. But not one of them could see beyond his or her own feelings. They finished their dinner in silence.

Mom carried the dishes to the sink. "I'll leave these until later. Delbert, bring me my laundry from out back. I need to set a while." She settled down on the couch to wait for the laundry.

Jeremy flopped down in the arm chair with a diving magazine he'd bought on the boardwalk, but he could not concentrate on it. He wondered how long he could get by before Mom and Pop found out about the job. He was dumb to have agreed to work where she did. Even if he kept riding the bus each day, she was bound to find out about it.

He could hear Mom now if she knew: "You wanting to

be a big-time ocean scientist (she'd have forgotten oceanographer) and can't even keep a job!"

And Pop: "There's no place in this world for a man who can't work, son."

Maybe if he found another job, it would go a little easier on him. But the boardwalk jobs would be all sewn up by now. And the jobs inland? The thought made him weary.

"Jeremy! Come out here!" Pop's voice was sharp.

Mom looked up in surprise. Jeremy got up and went to the backyard.

"What's this?" Pop pointed to the light Jeremy had put up.

"Oh, I meant to tell you about that," answered Jeremy, wondering why Pop was so angry. "It's an outside light. I thought it would be a good idea."

"Outside light, my foot! That's the old kitchen light."

"Pop, I know it looks a little weird, but I didn't think you'd care—"

"Boy, that's not meant for an outside light. You know that. What happens when it rains and water leaks in there?"

Jeremy didn't answer.

"Short out. Could start a fire," Pop answered, "or shock the daylights out of you! Don't do a job halfway like this, boy. And look at this wire—don't you remember, I told you always use that insulated wire outside—"

"Pop, you never told me anything!"

"I been over electrical work—"

"With Tyler! You taught Tyler! You never showed me anything about it!"

Pop stared at him, dumbfounded.

"The only reason I know about it at all is from watching Tyler."

"I—I guess it was Tyler," Pop said after a moment.

"I'll go unscrew the fuse and take it down," Jeremy said quietly.

When he went into the living room, Mom was just hanging up the phone. She turned and faced him. "Jeremy, that was Lottie Jones."

He stopped and looked at her. Lottie Jones. Mom's friend from the Seaside cafeteria.

"She said there was some trouble at the hospital with you today."

"Yes." Quickly he tried to think of a way to ease the situation, but he didn't know how much Lottie knew or had told Mom.

Pop had trailed in behind him. "What kind of trouble?"

"Said Jeremy attacked a patient!"

They both stared at him in disbelief.

"I didn't attack him exactly," Jeremy explained. "He was really giving me a bad time, and I went to grab him. An aide grabbed me and that made it look really bad."

"I never knew you to start a fight, son," said Pop.

"Jeremy, don't you know you can get in big trouble laying a hand on a patient? And you being a minor, it would all come back on us."

"It had been a really bad morning. The guy I worked with tried to kill himself over the weekend."

"Does Mr. Fielding know what you did?"

Jeremy nodded. "I had to go report to him."

Mom pursed her lips. "I s'pose he's suspended you."

"He was going to." Jeremy hesitated. "But I quit."

"You quit!"

Pop stepped forward. "Look here. I held back on this, but now I'll say it. I didn't wholly agree with you quitting the first job. Now how do you expect to find work when you've quit two jobs?"

"Jeremy, you should've taken your punishment," said Mom. "Now I want you to call Mr. Fielding and ask him can you still come back after your time's done. Tell him you'll straighten up."

"I can't do that, Mom."

"And why not?" Her voice was rising.

"Because I can't take it there!" Frustration held him now. He wanted to grab her and shake her into understanding, but instead he stood there, trembling. "I don't know that I wouldn't do the same thing again tomorrow!"

"Don't you shout at me! That's a mind-weakness, like I was telling you. You got to fight it—"

"Angela was right!" Jeremy burst out. "I can't do anything right around here. You never really hear me! You never understand!"

"Oh, that's what Angela thinks, is it?" She reached up and swept the school pictures off the shelf. "Well, Angela and Tyler don't belong here no more!" she shouted. "I'm giving up on them like they gave up on me. I'm sorry I loved them!" Then she placed Jeremy's picture on the top shelf and turned to point her finger at him. "You, though! I got hope in you, Jeremy, to be different. Don't you let me down!"

Under the burden of her pronouncement, a wave of

protest swelled up in his heart. How could she just wipe them out of her life with one angry swipe of her hand? And why was it he was expected to carry the banner of success for her when everyone else had failed? Did she think it was only she that had suffered?

"Mom, lay off me!" he yelled. "I don't know how to be different or the same. I don't even know how to be myself!"

8

Ꭹ y the time he reached the beach, he was breathless.
The sound of the screen door banging shut and Mom
yelling, "Jeremy, you come back here!" was still echoing
in his mind. He threw himself down on the sand and
closed his eyes.

It was a good time to be on the beach. There were no
Frisbees flying around, no children running and laughing, throwing sand. Just a few people quietly strolling
along. The sky was that in-between gray, and the moon,
edging up, was pale and ghostly.

With his eyes closed and the beach beneath him mold-
ing itself to the contours of his body, he felt a oneness
with the universe. He was but a speck on a slowly turn-

ing planet spinning through all eternity amid moons and stars and planets in a great black void. There was no Mom or Pop there. No Tyler. No Angela. No Seaside Hospital.

Then he heard a familiar voice somewhere above him. It drifted down from a place seemingly light-years away and called him back into consciousness. He raised himself on one elbow and peered up at Gina.

"Is this a private beach or may I use a little square of it?"

"Help yourself."

She dropped down on the sand beside him. "No offense, Jer, but you look terrible."

He sat up, rubbing his forehead with the heels of his hands. "I guess it's been the worst day of my life—well, second worst."

"You want to talk about it?"

"No. I'm afraid I'd start screaming."

Neither of them spoke, but looked down at the water. The waves were big and frothy. If I dove in there now, Jeremy mused, I'd just bob around like a buoy. Wouldn't even fight those waves.

"Jeremy, everything's going really bad for me, too. Sunday we finally drove down to Kitty Hawk like Dad wanted. He and Mom got into this big fight and they wanted *me* to referee it—to choose between them!"

"What did you do?"

She picked up a shell and tossed it away. "I told them not to pull me into their stupid fights. I said I couldn't stand either one of them anymore. And I can't, Jeremy. I really can't. When we got back, Dad started packing. He

said we were all going back to Maryland. I packed, too."
She pulled a small knapsack out from behind her back.
"But I'm not going back there with them. No way."

"What are you going to do?"

"I thought I'd hitchhike to Norfolk. It's a big city. I figure I can get a waitress job or something. I was hoping to
see you first, though."

"You're going tonight? Alone?"

"Yeah. Unless—you'd like to come."

Angela had said he should do it, now here was another
invitation! It seemed like forces were conspiring to give
him a message. And that message was clear: "Get out,
now, while you can!" And why not? He didn't have to be
Jeremy Chase, the suicide's brother. He didn't have to go
home and face Mom and Pop again. He could go to Norfolk and be Jeremy Chase, person. Person with no past.

He leaned over and hugged Gina. "Yeah! I'll go. You'll
be safer hitching with me along. I can get a job, too. Construction, maybe. We can help each other!"

Gina jumped up. "Come on. Let's go before it gets any
darker. You need to go home and get anything first?"

"No. I don't need anything." He reached in his
pocket. "I've got ten dollars. I'm not going home again!"

Gina had thought to stash a marker in her knapsack.
They pulled a piece of cardboard out of a dumpster and
wrote NORFOLK in bold, dark letters.

Their first ride, with a couple of teenage guys, let them
off right by the interstate highway. Darkness was falling
quickly now, and Jeremy was glad that he had on a pale-
yellow T-shirt, which made them visible in the headlights
of approaching cars. They stood just beyond the ramp,

holding their cardboard sign. Gina, standing by his side, was the first good thing that had happened all day.

"Do you think you'll ever go home?" Jeremy asked her.

"I'm not sure there'll be a home to go to and right now I don't care if I ever see either of them again. What about you? Will you go back?"

"Maybe. Someday. When I've made it." He pictured himself in expensive jeans and western boots. Maybe he'd have a motorcycle then. He'd roll into town. "Hi, Mom, Pop. How's it going? Thought I'd breeze in and drop off a hundred." He'd take the roll of bills out of his pocket and watch Mom and Pop, their eyes bulging. "We should have believed in you, Jeremy," Mom would say. "We're sorry." Jeremy smiled to himself. "Oh, no, put down the sign, Gina—the cops!"

It was too late. The turning light flashed red in their faces as the squad car rolled to a stop just beyond them.

"Oh, God," breathed Gina. "What'll they do?"

"I don't know. Put the sign in your knapsack." He squeezed her hand. "Be cool. I'll talk to them."

The officer, straightening his hat, came out of the car and walked up to them. "You kids see the sign?"

"What sign, sir?"

"On the ramp. No hitchhiking."

"Oh. We were going to Sand Dune. I guess we'll find another way."

"Your sign said 'Norfolk,' son. You're runaways, aren't you?"

Gina, despite the warmth of the night, was shivering. She moved closer to Jeremy.

"You're cold," the officer observed. "Come and sit down in the car."

"Officer, if we promise not to hitchhike, could we just go?" asked Jeremy.

"Son, you're in violation of the law. There's no hitch-hiking in Baxter Beach or on the interstate. What's more, you're trying to cross a state line, which makes you look like runaways to me. You'd best come sit in the car."

They followed the officer to the car and sat down in the backseat. The officer turned in his seat to look at them. He flicked on the inside light.

Outside, cars were whizzing by on the highway. Jeremy felt like he was trapped on a stage. He could almost feel the eyes of passersby, peering in, wondering who he was, why he had been picked up. And all he and Gina wanted was peace, to get away and live without constant harassment. Why were such simple things so difficult to attain?

"Where are you kids from?" asked the officer.

"Right here," said Jeremy. "Baxter Beach."

"How old are you?"

"Eighteen."

The officer squinted at Jeremy. "Eighteen, huh? How come every runaway I pick up is eighteen? Your girl friend here—I wouldn't put her past fourteen or fifteen. Son, did you know it's a criminal charge for you to take her across a state line if you're eighteen?"

Jeremy did not answer.

"Okay now, listen. I'm going to have to take you kids into the station. We're going to call your folks and have them come get you. I'll need some names."

Jeremy and Gina glanced at each other. "I'm Jeremy and this is Gina."

"Right. Now how about some last names."

Jeremy laid a silencing hand on Gina's arm and did not answer.

The officer sighed. "You're going to make this hard, aren't you? I'm going to give you two this ride to think things over. You can cooperate and we can have this thing done with and you home safe in about an hour. Or I can charge you with hitchhiking on the interstate and put you in lockup with a drunk and a thief or two 'til we figure out who you are. And then, of course, there'd be court."

He started up the car and pulled onto the highway. Was this the officer who took Tyler to the hospital, Jeremy wondered, with Tyler cruising along, looking out this same window, worrying about what lay ahead. Had he searched that same door for the missing button he could pull up and jump to freedom? But probably he had been handcuffed—had half lain there, his thoughts and emotions rioting within him, the metal tightening against his wrists as he twisted them.

In moments they were pulling up beside the station house on Second Street. The officer opened the back door to let them out.

"What do you think we should do?" Gina whispered.

Jeremy took her hand and shrugged. "Tell them, I guess." We could run for it, Jeremy thought, but that officer would come lumbering after and wrestle one of us to the ground. It would probably be Gina, and Jeremy knew he couldn't leave her there.

The little station was quiet when they went in. The desk sergeant set down his coffee mug. "Tom, whatcha got? These two knock over a bank?"

"This is Jeremy and Gina. Found'em heading north on the interstate—by thumb. They were having some trouble remembering their last names, but I think their memories might have improved."

"Okay, who'll be first?" asked the desk sergeant. "Young lady?"

"My name's Gina Peterson. I'm staying at the Wander Inn on Windy Lane with my folks. Room number seventeen."

The desk sergeant wrote the information down and turned to Jeremy.

"Jeremy Chase. Ten eighty-one Dunlaw Street."

The sergeant looked up. "You related to Tyler Chase?"

"His brother."

The two policemen exchanged glances. "Son," said the officer, "you better do some serious thinking before you put your folks through any more."

The dispatcher interrupted them. "Tom, you got a dune buggy heading south on the beach between Wright and Pinecrest."

The officer got up. "I'll see you later, Cal. And, Jeremy, you think it over," he said, and walked out.

The sergeant took Jeremy's phone number and then told them to sit and wait on the bench.

Gina's parents came first: her mother annoyed, her father embarrassed, both anxious to get out of the station. They barely acknowledged Jeremy, so that Jeremy wondered if they even realized they had been together. Gina looked helpless and wistful as she left with them. "I'll try to see you tomorrow on the boardwalk," she whispered. But Jeremy wondered if her parents wouldn't whisk her back to Maryland now.

Jeremy rested his forehead in the heels of his hands and waited. The desk sergeant was busy with a boozed-up old guy another officer had brought in. The dispatcher was pouring the last grimy-looking dregs from the coffeepot into a stained mug.

Outside the station door there was a patch of sparkling stars above. Just beyond the door, if he slipped out quietly in this moment of distraction, the sky would burst into a broad expanse of blackness and sparkles. The ocean, wide and waiting. The interstate laid out like an endless ribbon, leading to a million unknown towns, north and south.

Somewhere Mom and Pop were making their way through the darkness to the police station, again. Why were they taking so long? Pop had probably gone to work. Mom had taken the call, then. Did she start screaming, like she had with Tyler? Did she settle down long enough to hear that he wasn't dead, only trying to run away?

If he ran far enough, fast enough, he could get away. From what, he asked himself and knew the answer— them—and their fears that he would follow Tyler. For a moment he imagined his lifeless body washing up on the shore, the horrified sunbathers gathering around, his mother running across the sand in her white oxfords, screaming.

Jeremy got up and went into the men's room. Could they really push him to that? Angela thought so. Mom blamed Pop. Pop blamed Mom. Jeremy blamed himself. He leaned against the wall and looked up at the high square window. A circle of blame.

But Tyler was crazy. Tyler *was* crazy. Clearly crazier than Donnie, who also had tried to kill himself. Anybody who would sit like that for hours, who would burn live frogs . . . that talk of a power. . . . Nothing the family said could have changed that. Even Donnie said there were times you couldn't talk to a person. And if they couldn't have talked him out of craziness, well, then they couldn't have talked him into it. It was just the way he was—all on his own and by himself.

Suddenly something shook Jeremy from within. His eyes burned. The first sob was like an animal cry, and then he sank down to his knees and gave himself over to it.

When it was done he got up slowly, wiping his face dry with his hands. He was exhausted, yet there was another feeling, a feeling of lightness, freedom.

"Chase, you in here?" The bathroom door creaked open.

"Yeah."

The desk sergeant stepped in. "You all right?"

"Yes, sir. I'm all right."

"Your folks are here. They're waiting in an office. Your mother—she's pretty upset."

Jeremy nodded and started for the office. He hesitated at the door. Then he opened it. Pop had his arms around Mom. Her white handkerchief was wound around her fingers. When they saw him, his parents separated, and faced him.

"Jeremy, how could you do this—bring this shame to us again?" Mom's eyes were puffy, her forehead lined with worry.

"I'm sorry, Mom."

"Everybody looking at us—the dead boy's mother and father. Now the runaway's parents. I can't hold my head up."

Jeremy sighed. Mom, so concerned about how things looked! As if making Tyler's part of the room look normal would make Tyler normal. And as if marching through the days like a dutiful son would make Jeremy okay, no matter what he felt or thought.

"Jeremy, you scared the hell out of your mother," said Pop.

"When the police called, it was just like when Tyler—"

"Forget about Tyler!" Jeremy shouted.

"Forget! How can I forget—any of us forget? Your own brother!"

"Yes! My brother! Not me! Tyler—not Jeremy! We're not the same!"

"It's just that I was afraid that—you always—"

"Bury him, Mom! He's gone!"

She sank down in a chair, covering her face with her handkerchief. "Whatever I do, it doesn't seem right. Angela—you all—think I'm to blame, don't you?"

What a sorry bunch they were, Jeremy thought, all feeling so guilty, enslaved to that guilt. He went to her side. "Tyler's mind wasn't right. I understand that now."

"Delbert—"

Pop laid a hand on Mom's shoulder. "There's things

we all might've done, I guess," he said slowly. "But it might not have made a lick of difference to him." Rubbing the back of his neck, he turned to Jeremy. "Son, I been thinking how I taught Tyler that electrical work and thought it was you. I feel real bad about that. Seems like you being the second son missed out on a lot."

"Well, there's still time," Jeremy said after a moment.

"Yes," agreed Pop quickly. "There's time all right."

"Mom, Pop, let's go home, okay?"

Mom struggled to her feet and hugged him. "Jeremy's right. Let's go on home."

9

The next morning he awoke to the aroma of bacon and freshly brewed coffee. He stretched out one arm, turning the clock's face toward him. Mom was still home. He could hear Pop's voice, too. He pulled the sheet up over his bare shoulder and lay quietly. He felt sore and achy all over, as if every muscle had been tensed.

Last night, when they'd come home, he'd noticed that the glass that had been broken when Angela's picture was swept off the shelf had been cleaned up. Angela and Tyler's pictures were back on the shelf beside his. It had just been anger, then—an anger she'd regretted.

He threw back the sheet and swung his legs to the floor. Across from him was still the gaping space where

Tyler's bed had been. He got up and pushed his desk into the space. Then he went to the closet to get his jeans from the hook. His cemetery clothes were hanging there, clean and pressed. He looked at them a moment and then moved them to the back of the closet. He wouldn't be going back to the cemetery. Oh, maybe once a year or so. He couldn't, wouldn't forget Tyler, just wouldn't carry him around like a burden anymore. That didn't help anyone.

He pulled on his clothes and went into the kitchen. Pop was sitting at the table with a cup of coffee, but they had been waiting breakfast for him.

"Good morning," he said.

"Mornin', Jeremy," they answered.

"What's everybody doing home?"

"We thought we'd take the day off and spend it with you," said Mom, "if you didn't have plans."

"Oh. That's nice. I didn't have any plans." I would have been in Norfolk with Gina, he thought. That seems so long ago. He wondered if she was on her way back to Maryland now. He reached in his pocket and felt the little square of paper on which she'd written her address last night.

"Sit down, honey, and start your grapefruit," Mom said. "I'll have your eggs in a minute."

"Big breakfast."

"Well . . ."

Pop got up to fill his coffee cup. "Coffee, son?"

"No, thanks, Pop." He dug his spoon into the grapefruit. They really are trying, thought Jeremy. Trying to start over. Maybe we can . . .

He thought of Angela, sitting in her little apartment at

the other end of town. He thought of the new life within her. Maybe what she really wanted was to start over. Mom and Pop coming after her—even though she said no—would have proved how much they cared. But they hadn't realized. A year had passed, a year without new fights, a year of missing, of regretting. Maybe it was enough to allow them to start over.

Mom set a plate of eggs, bacon and grits in front of him and in a moment returned with hers and Pop's.

"What did you all want to do today?" asked Jeremy.

"We didn't have anything special in mind," said Mom. "Could go for a drive."

"I been thinking about building a screen porch," Pop put in. "Your mother's been wanting one. We could get started on that."

"Well, I was thinking about Angela," said Jeremy. "I thought it'd be nice to go visiting. Have a little reunion."

"Honey, your sister is done with us. She made that plain. It's going to be just you, Pop, and me now."

It would be that way, Jeremy realized, if no one pushed for it to change. Mom and Pop wouldn't do it. Angela wouldn't. And yet they all really wanted it. He wondered, if he got them all together, would they make it work?

"Mom, Angela was angry then. But that was a long time ago. Things change."

"You think she wants to see us?"

"Sure she does."

Pop leaned forward on his elbows. "She knows where we are. Why don't she come, then?"

"She's scared—just like you all. Scared you don't want her." Jeremy felt the shakiness of his position, but he couldn't back down. *Someone* had to take charge and get them all together. And if they blew it with each other—well, at least he'd have tried.

Mom and Pop exchanged a glance. "It would be nice to have us all together again," said Mom. "The four of us."

"Why don't you call her up, Jeremy?" suggested Pop. "Invite her home. I can't see your mother having to go across town after how Angela left."

"I don't think she has a phone," said Jeremy. "Besides, then you wouldn't get to see her place. You'd like to see where she's living, wouldn't you, Mom?"

"Yes," Mom said slowly. She looked at Pop and smiled. "I could wear my blue dress and that necklace she gave me—the one with the shells. That'd please her."

"If you're sure that's what you want to do, Lydia."

"Yes. Jeremy's been to see her. He knows how she is. And . . . I *do* miss her."

Pop nodded. "I know. I've missed her, too. After breakfast we'll go, then."

The clouds were gathered in dark gray knots when they left the house and as they drove, a light rain began to fall. Jeremy hoped he hadn't built Mom and Pop up too much. Even though Angela wanted to see them down deep, she probably wouldn't exactly jump for joy. If it didn't work, all three of them would blame him. And what if she wasn't even home? Or what if Todd was there? He hadn't even thought of that. They'd hit the roof when they found out about Todd—and the baby. But above all, she was their daughter. They were family. They'd have to see that, wouldn't they?

He saw Angela's building ahead of them and leaned

(115)

forward. "That white building on the right, Pop. Park by the steps—she's on the second floor."

"Kinda peely-looking," said Mom.

"Lydia, remember our first place?" Pop asked suddenly.

"Yes!" She laughed. "That old apartment over the laundromat. How it shook on Saturday mornings!"

They started up the steps, Mom clutching the strings of her plastic rain hat beneath her chin.

Jeremy knocked on the door and stepped aside. Maybe there was no one home. Maybe that would be better. They could leave a note. Then Angela would know they tried. Angela and Mom always got into arguments so easily. If only they would both try. . . .

"Knock again, Jeremy," said Mom.

He knocked. From within they heard Angela call, "Coming!" Then footsteps and the door opened. "Mom! Everyone!" she exclaimed, looking at each of them.

For a moment she and Mom stood wavering and speechless before each other. Then, reaching out across the many months, they embraced.

Gail Radley, the author of *The Night Stella Hid the Stars,* was born in Boston and was raised in the suburbs of Washington, D.C. Eager to experience another way of life, she worked as a store clerk in Louisiana, a waitress in Tennessee, and a volunteer in a children's program in New Mexico. She then attended Boston University but left two years later and once again drifted around the country—working as an EKG technician, a health assistant, and a teacher's aide in a program for mentally retarded children. She now lives with her husband and their two children in a rural area of Virginia. *The World Turned Inside Out* is her second novel. Her first was *Nothing Stays the Same Forever.*